THE WORLD OF NORM

NORM

MAY BE RECYCLED

ORCHARD BOOKS

First published in Great Britain in 2016 by The Watts Publishing Group

1 3 5 7 9 10 8 6 4 2

Text © Jonathan Meres 2016
Illustrations © Donough O'Malley 2016

The moral rights of the author and illustrator have been asserted.

A CIP catalogue record for this book
is available from the British Library.

ISBN 978 1 40834 484 2

Printed and bound in Great Britain by CPI Group (UK) Ltd, Croydon, CR0 4YY

The paper and board used in this book are from well-managed forests
and other responsible sources.

Orchard Books
An imprint of

Hachette Children's Group
Part of The Watts Publishing Group Limited
Carmelite House
50 Victoria Embankment
London EC4Y 0DZ
An Hachette UK Company
www.hachette.co.uk
www.hachettechildrens.co.uk

JONATHAN MERES

THE WORLD OF
NORM
MAY BE RECYCLED

ORCHARD

To librarians everywhere,
for whom my admiration is beyond categorisation.

CHAPTER 1

Norm knew it was going to be one of those days when he woke up and nothing happened. Zilch. Nada. Nothing whatso-flipping-ever. He just opened his eyes and, well...that was it, really. As far as Norm could tell, he wasn't anywhere he **shouldn't** have been. And as far as he could tell, he wasn't about to be doing anything that he **shouldn't** have been doing. Everything was perfectly normal. Whatever **that** meant. Norm was simply lying in bed, scratching his bum. Not that his bum actually **needed** scratching. He just **felt** like scratching it. So he did.

But even **before** he'd opened his eyes, it had occurred to Norm that the house was a bit quiet. Actually it was more than just a **bit** quiet. It was **eerily** quiet. Almost **spookily** quiet, in fact. Not that Norm believed in ghosts or any of that kind of stuff, of course. But that wasn't the point. The point was that it was quiet enough to hear a pin drop. Though why Norm would have actually **wanted** to drop a pin and listen to it in the first place was another matter entirely. He'd have only had to pick it up again afterwards. And as far as Norm was concerned, picking stuff up from the floor was **way** too much like hard work and a complete waste of energy. Energy which could be put to **far** better use. Preferably biking. And

6

because it was **Saturday**, biking was precisely what Norm intended to do once he'd got up and stuffed his face with a bowl of supermarket own-brand Coco Pops. Not that there was much choice when it came to types or brands of Coco Pops these days. Or **any** choice for that matter.

Not since his dad had been made redundant and his mum had had to get a part time job at a cake shop. But that wasn't the point either. The point was that, as far as Norm could tell, something was definitely going on. Or rather, several things that **normally** went on definitely **weren't** going on at the moment. Things like slamming doors and yapping dogs. Or strictly speaking, slamming doors and yapping **dog**, because they only actually had one dog. Which, in Norm's opinion, was still one more dog than was necessary.

It really was quite extraordinary how much noise and smell a relatively small dog like John the half-Polish cockapoo could generate. It was the same

with Norm's two little brothers, Brian and Dave. It was quite extraordinary just how much noise and smell **they** could generate, too. Not that it took much noise or smell to fill a house **that** small, of course. Their old house hadn't been **particularly** big. But compared to the glorified hamster cage they now lived in, it seemed like some kind of fairy-tale palace. As for the thickness of the walls? If they'd been any thinner they'd have been transparent. Never mind being able to **hear** someone putting socks on in the next room, you could practically see them doing it. So the fact that Norm **couldn't** hear or smell his brothers **or** the dog, immediately made him wonder. Was he all alone? He looked at the clock on the wall. It was ten thirty. Presumably ten thirty in the morning. If it was ten thirty at night then something really **was** going on! Or had already gone on. If not then how come his mum or dad hadn't woken him up yet? Because they normally would have done by now.

Norm stopped scratching his bum for a moment and listened. The silence was almost deafening. There was only one thing for it. He was going to have to actually get up and go and investigate for himself. And as soon as he'd finished checking Facebook and browsed a few bike websites and looked at a couple of new biking videos on YouTube, that was **precisely** what Norm intended to do.

CHAPTER 2

It took some time for Norm to check Facebook **and** for him to drool over the latest bikes on his favourite sites. It always did. And, of course, there was no such thing as a **quick** look at biking videos on YouTube. There never was. Not for Norm there wasn't, anyway. Because one video soon led to another. And another. And another. And before Norm knew it – or rather, before Norm **would** have known it if he'd actually bothered to look at the clock again – it was ten past eleven. Presumably ten past eleven in the morning. Either way, everything was **still** spookily quiet. Something was **definitely** still going on. Or rather, something was definitely still **not** going on.

"Hello?" said Norm, from the top of the stairs.

But there was no reply.

"Hello?" said Norm again, this time a bit louder and this time from the bottom of the stairs.

But there was still no reply.

Funny, thought Norm as he poked his head into the front room like a turtle peering out of its shell. No one had **said** anything about going out. Or, at least, Norm couldn't remember anyone saying anything about going out, anyway. Then again there were some days Norm could barely remember his own **name**, let alone anyone else's. So it was hardly surprising if he couldn't remember whether someone had actually **said** something about going out or not. Either way it was beginning to look like he was all alone in the house. Not that Norm was particularly bothered if he was. Far from it. He wasn't in the **least** bit bothered at the prospect of being all by himself. He positively **welcomed** the prospect of being all by himself. Because at least then his brothers couldn't keep annoying him. And at least his parents couldn't keep banging on and on and telling him to flipping **do** stuff. Especially stuff that didn't actually **need** doing in the first flipping place. Which, in Norm's experience, meant pretty much anything and everything. And anyway there was no reason on earth why Norm **should** be freaked out just because no one else was in. It wasn't as if he was a **kid** any more. He was nearly **thirteen**, for Gordon Bennet's sake.

Norm's suspicions proved to be well founded, as he entered the kitchen to discover that there was no one there. Just as there hadn't been anyone in the front room either. Or the bathroom. Though quite why the rest of the family, including the dog, would all be in the **bathroom** at the same time was anybody's guess. And Norm didn't particularly **want** to guess. But that wasn't the point. The point was that it looked like Norm really **was** home alone.

Norm immediately did what any right-thinking kid in a similar position would do – headed straight for the fridge. What tasty treats and mouthwatering delights awaited him there? he wondered. A slice of leftover deep pan Margherita pizza from last night's takeaway, perhaps? Maybe some garlic bread too, if he was **really** lucky. And all washed down with a can of the finest own-brand cola that money could buy. Never mind that it was nowhere near lunchtime yet. Never mind that he hadn't even had breakfast. The own-brand Coco Pops could wait. Norm was going to quite literally fill his boots. Well, maybe not **literally** fill his boots. But he was definitely going to take full advantage of the situation. And besides, he wasn't even **wearing** boots.

It was only when Norm reached out to open the fridge that he noticed the note stuck on the door by a magnet in the shape of a cow. A note that said 'NORMAN' at the top, in large capital letters and underlined twice.

"Gordon flipping **Bennet**," muttered Norm quietly under his breath. Not that there was anyone there to hear him if he'd said it a bit louder. But it was almost as if his parents **knew** he'd make a beeline for the fridge as soon as he realised there was no one else in. It was so annoying, thought Norm. Because not only were they **right**, but he was now going to have to **read** the flipping note!

Norm read:

"Gone to the supermarket. Please hang the washing out and do the recycling. Love Mum. PS There's nothing in the fridge. That's why we've gone to the supermarket :D"

"WHAAAAAAAAAT?" roared Norm, like a tiger with toothache. Not that Norm had ever actually **heard** a tiger with toothache roar before. But that wasn't the point. The point was that his mum and dad weren't even here, but they'd **still** told him to **do** something. That wasn't just **unfair**.

It was unbe-flipping-*lievably* unfair! It was unfair on toast. It was unfair squared! And to top it all they'd left him with an empty fridge? How could they *do* that? What was he supposed to *eat*? The flipping *dog's* food?

Norm read the note again, but more slowly and deliberately. Just in *case* he'd skimmed over it a bit too quickly and hadn't quite grasped its meaning first time round. But sadly he *had*. He'd grasped its meaning only too well. It couldn't be interpreted any other way. And there was nothing about it that Norm didn't find incredibly and intensely irritating. Even the smiley face at the bottom made him want to flipping *scream*. Did his mum honestly think that that would somehow make the note *better*? Because if anything, it had the complete *opposite* effect. It was almost as if the smiley face was mocking him – poking *fun* at him!

Norm opened the fridge. Just in case his mum had been joking and the fridge was full, after all. In fact, just in case the whole flipping thing about the washing and the recycling was some kind of massive wind-up too, and everyone was suddenly going to leap out from under the table and yell, "SURPRISE!"

But it soon became clear to Norm that it **wasn't** a wind-up, massive or otherwise. There really was **nothing** in the fridge. At least nothing that looked even remotely edible, or didn't look like it belonged in some kind of science experiment. Given a choice, he actually **would** sooner eat dog food than some of **this** stuff.

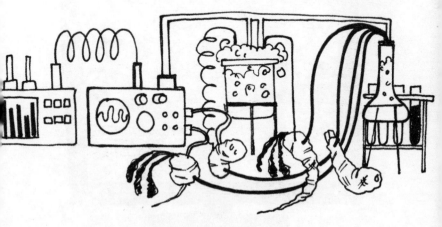

There was only one thing for it, thought Norm. He was just going to have to grit his teeth and get on with it. Much as he loathed the idea – and he loathed the idea very much indeed – he was actually going to have to hang the flipping washing out **and** do the flipping recycling. Who knew what terrible punishment his parents would inflict on him, if he didn't. Because, frankly, if they were cruel and heartless enough to leave him to fend for himself in a food-free house, like a contestant on some kind of weird reality TV show, then they were clearly capable of doing just about **anything**.

Like a condemned prisoner resigned to his fate, Norm sighed and closed the fridge door again. The sooner he got on with it, the sooner it would all be over. And anyway, thought Norm, trudging slowly towards the utility room, it was only hanging washing out. What was the worst thing that could actually **happen?**

CHAPTER 3

It took precisely forty-three seconds for Norm to find out what the worst thing that could happen was. Not that Norm had actually been timing it, of course. But that was how long it had taken for him to walk into the back garden, carrying the laundry basket, and start to peg stuff onto the clothes line.

"Hello, **Norman**!" said an instantly identifiable and, to Norm, instantly annoying voice.

Norm didn't need to turn round to know that it was Chelsea. So he didn't. Because there was only one person

who deliberately overemphasised his name as if it was the funniest thing she'd ever heard. And there was only one person who popped up over the fence if he so much as stuck his big toe out the flipping door.

"I said hello, **Norman**!" said Chelsea again.

"Heard you the flipping *first* time," muttered Norm through firmly gritted teeth.

"I know you're just ***pretending*** not to be pleased to see me," said Chelsea.

Was she **serious**? thought Norm. **Pretending** not to be pleased to see her? What was this? Some kind of flipping **game**? Did she think they were at **nursery**, or something? Because there was

no **pretending** about it, whatso-flipping-**ever**. Chelsea was genuinely the last person on Earth he wanted to see right now. Or ever, come to think of it.

"Are they yours?" said Chelsea with a nod towards the clothes line.

"Uh? What?" said Norm, who hadn't been paying much attention to what he'd been hanging out on the line. Actually that wasn't true. He hadn't been paying **any** attention to what he'd been hanging out on the line. Until now.

AAAAAARGH! thought Norm. Of **all** the things he could have been holding when Chelsea stuck her stupid face over the flipping fence, it just **had** to be a pair of his mum's frilly **pants**, didn't it? Flipping **typical**.

"I said are they **yours**?" said Chelsea.

"**No!**" said Norm as if this was the unlikeliest, most

outrageous question he'd ever heard in his life. "Course they're flipping not!"

"Are you sure, **Norman**?"

Norm sighed. He was pretty sure of **one** thing. Chelsea had just smashed her own personal record for the shortest time to wind him up. And **that** was saying something.

"How come you've gone red, then?"

"What?" said Norm.

"Well if they're not yours, how come you've gone red?" Chelsea grinned.

Gordon flipping **Bennet**, thought Norm. He **had** gone red. He could feel his face burning. And no flipping wonder, either. He was hanging his mum's pants out on the flipping washing line, for goodness sake!

"What are you up to?"

"Uh?" said Norm. "What does it **look** like I'm up to?"

"I mean what are you up to after you've **finished** doing that, silly!" said Chelsea.

"Oh, right," said Norm. "Some socks, maybe?"

"I mean after you've finished hanging the **washing** out!" said Chelsea.

"Doing the recycling."

"Lucky you," said Chelsea. "Living the dream."

More like living a flipping nightmare, thought Norm.

"And after that?"

Norm shrugged. "Dunno. Biking, probably. Why?"

"No particular reason, **Norman**," said Chelsea. "Just making polite conversation, that's all."

"Really annoying conversation more like," muttered Norm.

"What was that, Norman?"

"Nothing," said Norm.

"So in other words, you're doing the recycling and then you're going **cycling**!" said Chelsea.

Norm pulled a face. "What? Oh right. Yeah. Suppose so."

"Not bad, eh?" said Chelsea. "You can use that, if you want."

Norm thought for a moment. Why would he want to use that? Or anything else that Chelsea had ever said, for that matter. And anyway why couldn't she just leave him alone and let him get on with it? It was annoying enough already, having to do chores like he was some kind of domestic slave from the olden days. But having to do chores, with an *audience*? If you could actually call one person an audience. But that wasn't the point, thought Norm. The point was that he wished Chelsea would hurry up and disappear as quickly as she'd appeared. But the problem was she never flipping did. She always lurked and lingered like a bad smell. And it wasn't as if Norm could just open a window and let the smell out. He was outside already!

26

"Want a hand?" said Chelsea.

"Erm..." began Norm. But it was too late. Chelsea had already clambered over the fence and was busy delving into the laundry basket.

"But..."

"What?" Chelsea laughed. "I'm just trying to be helpful!"

Norm groaned. If Chelsea **really** wanted to be helpful, she'd climb back over the flipping fence and clear off.

"Now these **must** be yours," giggled Chelsea, producing a pair of boxer shorts and holding them in the air. "Please tell me those skid marks are part of the design – and not **actual** skid marks?"

"Gimme those here!" yelled Norm snatching them out of her hands again.

"Ah, so they **are** yours, then," said Chelsea.

Norm shrugged. "Might be."

Chelsea raised her eyebrows. "**Might** be?"

"It's none of your flipping business whose they are!" snapped Norm, finally losing the little bit of self-control he'd had to start with. "And if you must know – yes – the skid marks **are** part of the design. I got them from a biking website."

"All right, **Norman**!" said Chelsea. "Calm down!"

Calm **down**? thought Norm. That was easy for **her** to say! **She** wasn't the one who'd just had her pants waved around like a flipping flag for the whole flipping **neighbourhood** to see.

"Hi!" shrieked Brian and Dave, exploding into the garden like a whirlwind.

It wasn't very often that Norm was actually **glad** to see his brothers, but on this particular occasion he would have **happily** hugged them. Well, maybe not happily hugged them. Grudgingly hugged them, perhaps. And then gone for a shower straight afterwards to wash off the smell. But that wasn't the point. The point was that Brian and Dave suddenly appearing had come as something of a **relief**. Because Norm wasn't sure how much more of Chelsea he could take.

"We're back," said Brian.

"Obviously," said Dave.

Brian looked puzzled. "What?"

"Well obviously we're back," said Dave. "Otherwise we wouldn't be here, would we? We'd be somewhere else."

"Hmmm. I see what you mean," said Brian, stroking his chin.

Dave suddenly seemed to notice what Norm and Chelsea were actually doing. Or rather, **had** been doing until they'd showed up.

"Are you playing Mummies and Daddies?"

"NOOOOO!" blurted Norm as if this was the single most horrific idea he'd ever heard – and was ever likely **to** hear.

"Aw, they're adorable!" giggled Chelsea.

"You think so?" said Norm, still looking and sounding slightly flustered. "You should try living with them."

"Charming," said Dave.

"Shut up, you little freak," said Norm.

"Language," said Dave.

And to think, thought Norm, that only a few seconds ago he'd actually been **relieved** to see his brothers. Now it was business as usual. They were driving him up the flipping wall. Or driving him up the fence, anyway.

"Do you two **want** anything?"

Brian thought for a moment. "I want the new *Lord of the Rings* Lego."

"What?" said Norm.

"Hobbit Battle of Five Armies. It's awesome!"

"I don't think that's what Norman meant, Brian," said Dave. "Remember what Dad told us to tell him?"

"What? Oh right, yeah," said Brian. "You've got to come and help bring the shopping in, **Norman**."

"WHAAAAT?" bellowed Norm incredulously.

"He said you've got to go and help bring the shopping in, Norman!" said Chelsea.

Gordon flipping **Bennet**, thought Norm. He'd **heard** what Brian had said. He just couldn't quite **believe** what Brian had said. He'd actually got to go and help with the shopping? Seriously? On top of all the **other** chores he'd been given to do? This really **was** a wind-up. It **had** to be. Either that or Norm had accidentally travelled back to Victorian times and been reincarnated as a flipping butler. Which, knowing **his** luck, he probably flipping **had**.

"We're not joking," said Dave, as if he could read Norm's mind.

Be a pretty rubbish joke if they **were**, thought Norm, heading off.

"I'll just finish hanging out your pants then, shall I?" Chelsea grinned.

Whatever, thought Norm, disappearing into the house, the hysterical laughter of his two little brothers still ringing in his ears.

CHAPTER 4

"About time, too," said Norm's dad as Norm appeared in the kitchen with all the enthusiasm of a pig walking into a butcher's. "Where have you **been**?"

Where had he **been**? thought Norm. In the flipping garden, being ritually humiliated by his next door neighbour and driven up the wall by his flipping brothers! **That's** where he'd **been**.

"Well, Norman?"

"I've been hanging out the washing," said Norm.

Norm's dad looked at Norm for a moment. "You've only just **done** that?"

Norm nodded.

"Why didn't you do it earlier?"

"What?" said Norm.

"Pardon," said Norm's dad.

"What?" said Norm, a bit louder.

"I meant don't say **what**, say **pardon**!" said Norm's dad, the vein on the side of his head beginning to throb – a surefire sign that he was already getting stressed. Not that Norm noticed. Or *ever* seemed to notice, for that matter.

"So?" said Norm's dad.

"What?" said Norm. "I mean, pardon?"

"Why have you only *just* been hanging the washing out? If you'd done it when we left, it would have been almost *dry* by now!"

Norm shrugged. "I wasn't *awake* when you left."

"What do you *mean*, you weren't awake, Norman?"

Uh? thought Norm. Adults in general were weird. But his dad took weird to a whole new level. What part of *wasn't awake* did he not understand? How much clearer did Norm need to be? The *reason* he hadn't been awake when everyone had left for the supermarket earlier, was because he'd been *asleep*. Unless of course this was some kind of trick question. In which case, what was the correct answer?

"Mum **woke** you," said Norm's dad.

Norm pulled a face. "She did?"

"Yes. She **did**," said Norm's dad. "Have you done the recycling yet, by the way?"

"Not yet," said Norm.

"Not **yet**?" said Norm's dad. "What do you mean, not **yet**?"

Gordon flipping **Bennet**, thought Norm. First his dad didn't seem to understand the basic difference between being **asleep** and being **awake** – and now he didn't know what he meant when he said **not yet**? Honestly, it was like talking to a flipping jellyfish sometimes. If that wasn't too disrespectful to jellyfish.

"I'll take that as a 'no' then," said Norm's dad. "It was a silly question, I suppose."

A **silly** question? thought Norm. It was a flipping **ridiculous** question.

"What was?" said Norm's mum, coming in from the hall, a bulging shopping bag in each hand.

"What?" said Norm's dad.

Norm shot his dad a glance.

"Er, I mean, pardon?" said Norm's dad, quickly correcting himself.

"What was a silly question?" said Norm's mum.

"Whether Norman had done the recycling yet."

"I see," said Norm's mum, putting the bags down before turning to Norm. "And? Have you?"

"No, Mum," said Norm. "Not yet."

"*That* was why it was a silly question," said Norm's dad.

"Ah, I see," said Norm's mum. "And *why* haven't you done it yet, love?"

Norm shrugged. "Because I wasn't awake."

Norm's mum smiled. "Do you not remember me waking you?"

Norm sighed. All these stupid flipping questions. It was like being back in *school* all of a sudden. Except not quite so much fun. And anyway, what difference would it make if he *could* actually remember his mum waking him? None whatso-flipping-*ever*. So what was the point banging on and on and *on* about it? Because as far as Norm could see, there *wasn't* one.

"Norman!" said Norm's dad sternly. "Your mum

asked you a question!"

"Oh, it doesn't really matter," said Norm's mum, beginning to unpack the bags and put the shopping away. "We've got to hurry up."

"Why have we?" said Norm.

"Because they'll be here in half an hour," said Norm's mum, glancing at the digital clock on the cooker.

"Who will?" said Norm.

"Auntie Jem and Uncle Steve," said Norm's mum. "They're coming for lunch. I told you when I woke you, love."

"But..." began Norm.

"What?"

Norm had a horrible feeling that he knew the answer before he'd even asked the question. He could sense the storm clouds beginning to gather. Not *actual* storm clouds. Storm clouds inside his head, getting darker and darker. And any second now they were going to burst.

"Does that mean..."

"That your cousins are coming as well?" said Norm's mum. "Well, of course they are. I told you that, too!"

Norm stared at his mum. Even if he **had** been able to think of something to say, he wouldn't have been able to say it. But then it wasn't easy talking when you felt as if all the air had suddenly been sucked out of your lungs and you'd just been whacked around the head with an enormous sledgehammer.

"Norman?" said Norm's mum.

CROAK

"Yeah?" Norm just about managed to croak, like a toad with tonsillitis.

"What's wrong?"

What's **wrong**? thought Norm. Seriously? Did his mum even have to **ask**? Surely she knew that he'd rather have every meal, every day, for the rest of his life, with **Chelsea** than have so much as a single sandwich with his flipping **cousins**. His **perfect** flipping cousins. Who were always best at this, that and the other. Who were always winning things. Who were always doing stuff that no one else did. Who were always playing instruments he'd never even **heard** of. And who were always going to places he never knew even **existed**. They were

SO flipping annoying! And they were going to be here in half an **hour**? Was it too late to emigrate? wondered Norm. He didn't care where to. The further away the flipping better, as far as **he** was concerned. Because the mere **thought** of being cooped up in the same room as his perfect cousins was enough to make Norm lose his lunch. And he hadn't even **had** lunch yet!

"Answer your mother!" snapped Norm's dad, the vein on the side of his head beginning to throb faster and faster. Not that Norm noticed. But luckily his mum did. And she was quick to step in before things could escalate even further.

"I know they can be a little...oh, what's the word?"

Norm could think of **several** words to describe his cousins. But under the circumstances he decided it was probably best to bite his tongue and let his mum come up with one herself. Which she eventually did.

"Challenging?"

Challenging? thought Norm. Hmmm, well, that was certainly **one** way of putting it. But unlike the challenges he **usually** faced – most of which involved hurtling down hillsides on his bike as fast as possible, trying to avoid smashing into rocks and trees and various other obstacles – the prospect of this **particular** challenge filled Norm with a **real** sense of dread. Because at least when he was on his bike, he was in control of the situation. Well, more or less in control of the situation anyway. OK, so sometimes he fell off, or hit something, or swerved to **avoid** hitting something. But he knew that that was one of the risks and he was OK with it. If he **wasn't**, then he would have taken up something a little **less** dangerous instead, like embroidery, or flipping flower arranging.

And besides, nobody **made** Norm go biking. He went biking **voluntarily**. Because he actually **wanted** to do it. How else was he ever going to become World Mountain Biking Champion, if he didn't practise? But a visit from his cousins? His perfect flipping cousins? That was different. That was way, **way** different. Because it was out of Norm's control. He couldn't possibly predict what was going to happen. Apart from the fact that they'd wind him up more than Chelsea and his brothers could manage to, combined. They were bound to. They always flipping **did**. But unlike when he was **biking**, Norm couldn't simply put a helmet and some kneepads on and hope for the best.

"Look, son," said Norm's dad a little more calmly. "At the end of the day, they're family."

Yeah, so? thought Norm. That didn't mean he had to actually *like* them, did it? And anyway he still only had his parents' word for it that his cousins really *were* family. He'd never seen it in writing. Frankly, he still wasn't entirely convinced that they were a hundred per cent *human*, let alone that he was biologically *related* to them.

"Your dad's right, love," said Norm's mum.

Norm looked at his mum. "But..."

"What?" said Norm's mum.

"I'm going biking, with Mikey."

"Correction," said Norm's dad. "You **were** going biking, with Mikey."

Norm sighed.

"And you can stop doing that, for a start!" said Norm's dad.

"Doing what?" said Norm.

"All that huffing and puffing."

Seriously? thought Norm. He'd just been told that he could no longer do the one thing in the whole wide world that he loved doing the **most**, because the three people in the whole wide world he wanted to see the **least** were about to pay a visit – and he couldn't even **sigh**? What did they **expect** him to do? Run down the street, whooping and hollering and pulling flipping party poppers?

"You'd better get a move on," said Norm's dad.

"With what?" said Norm.

"What do you mean, with what?" said Norm's dad.

Gordon flipping **Bennet**, thought Norm. Not **again**. What was **wrong** with his dad? Had he accidentally taken a **stupid** pill or something?

"Bringing the shopping in from the car, love," said Norm's mum, yet again attempting to act as the peacemaker.

"And once you've done that you can do the recycling!" added Norm's dad. "And anything else your mum asks you to do!"

Norm **started** to sigh, but managed to stifle it just in time. It wasn't like his day could get much worse – but even so, he knew that if he wasn't careful, it flipping well **would**.

"FINISHED!" shrieked Brian and Dave, suddenly appearing in the doorway, holding the empty laundry basket between them.

Norm's dad looked at them for a moment, before turning slowly and fixing his gaze on his eldest son.

"What?" said Norm.

"Don't you dare 'what' me, Norman!"

"But..."

"And don't 'but' me, either," said Norm's dad. "I thought you said that you'd been hanging out the washing?"

Norm shrugged. "I did."

"No you didn't," said Norm's dad irritably. "Your brothers did."

"Uh?" said Norm. "No, I mean I **did** say that, Dad. That I'd been hanging out the washing."

Norm's dad was beginning to look thoroughly confused.

"I didn't say I'd **finished** doing it," said Norm.

"Why not?" said Norm's dad.

Norm pulled a face. "Because you didn't **ask** me."

"What?" said Norm's dad. "No, I meant **why** didn't you finish hanging it out, **yourself**?"

"Because you said I had to come inside and help!" said Norm, wondering why adults couldn't just say what they meant the first time instead of talking in flipping riddles all the time. Because this was starting to do his nut in. In fact never mind **starting** to do his nut in, thought Norm, it had

already done his nut in.

"He's right," said Norm's mum, turning to his dad. "You did."

"I hung your boxers out, Dad," said Brian.

"What?" said Norm's dad.

"The ones with the picture of the—" But before Brian could finish, there was an almighty clap of thunder outside.

"Gordon flipping Bennet!" shrieked Norm as John shot into the kitchen and hid under the table, whimpering.

"Language," said Dave.

"Shut up, you little freak," hissed Norm.

"It's just thunder," said Brian.

"Yeah, I know," said Norm nonchalantly. Or at least as nonchalantly as he could with his heart still beating twice as fast as it usually did.

"Scaredy cat!" Dave laughed.

"I'm not scared," said Norm.

"Good," said his dad. "In that case you'd better get out there and bring the washing in again."

"WHAAAAAT?" bawled Norm like a baby. "JUST *ME*?"

"Yes. Just you," said Norm's dad. "And quick.

Because it looks like it's going to pour it down in a minute."

"THAT IS **SO** UNFAIR!"

"Just do it, love. There's a good boy," said Norm's mum.

"And **then** bring the shopping in and do the recycling," said Norm's dad.

"Yeah, Norman." Brian grinned.

"Yeah, Norman." Dave grinned.

Give me flipping **strength**, thought Norm, setting off for the garden once again.

"Bet you're glad you're not going biking now, love," said Norm's mum as the first raindrops began beating against the window pane.

"Never been happier," muttered Norm, disappearing through the door.

CHAPTER 5

By the time Norm had brought the washing **and** the rest of the shopping in, he looked **and** felt a bit like a drowned rat. Not that Norm actually knew what it felt like to be a drowned rat, or, for that matter, a non-drowned rat. But that wasn't the point. The point was, his dad's weather forecast had turned out to be entirely accurate. It **had poured** down. In fact it hadn't just poured down, it had abso-flipping-lutely **peed** down. Indeed, it still **was** peeing down and looked like it might **continue** to pee down for some time. Not that that would stop Auntie Jem and Uncle Steve from coming, worse flipping luck, thought Norm, squelching into the kitchen with the last two carrier bags. They'd come by flipping speedboat if necessary, towing his perfect cousins behind on water skis. Because knowing his perfect cousins, they were probably world champion flipping water skiers!

"Don't just stand there dripping all over the floor, love!" said Norm's mum, putting a dish into the oven.

"Uh?" said Norm. "Where am I supposed to drip, then?"

"Give me those," said Norm's dad. "And don't be so cheeky!"

"But—" began Norm, doing as he was told and handing over the carrier bags.

"And don't answer **back**!"

"But—" began Norm again.

"I said don't answer back!" said his dad, cutting him off.

Norm sighed. Of **all** the annoying things his dad regularly said – and there were **plenty** of them – 'Don't answer back' had to be right up there at the top of the list of **the** most annoying. Not that there actually **was** a list of course. But if there were, it would be. And anyway it was a perfectly reasonable question, wasn't it? Where **was** he supposed to drip? On the flipping **ceiling**?

"Have you done the recycling yet?"

Norm looked at his dad frantically unpacking the shopping and putting it away in various cupboards and drawers.

"Well?" said Norm's dad. "**Have** you?"

"Am I allowed to answer back?" said Norm.

Norm's dad took a deep breath, before exhaling again, slowly and noisily. "Yes, you're allowed."

"Not yet," said Norm.

"What do you mean, not yet?" said his dad.

"I mean I haven't done the recycling yet."

"Well, in that case, what are you waiting for?" said Norm's dad, the vein on the side of his head immediately beginning to throb again. Not that Norm noticed. Again.

"But..."

"But **what**?" said Norm's dad, his voice getting fractionally higher – **another** surefire sign that he was getting stressed. And another one which, for some reason, Norm never seemed to detect.

"Why can't someone **else** do it?"

"Because **you** were the one who was **asked** to do it, Norman! **That's** why!"

"And anyway," said Norm's mum, "**we're** all dry and **you're** already soaked."

"Yeah, Norman!" Brian laughed as he set the table. "You look like you've wet yourself!"

"Very funny, Brian," said Norm.

"Thanks," said Brian, looking quite pleased with himself.

"I think Norman was being sarcastic," said Dave,

folding paper napkins into neat little triangles.

"Oh right," said Brian.

"Go on, love," said Norm's mum, glancing at the clock. "And then you'd better go and get changed. Because Brian's right. You **do** look like you've wet yourself. And they'll be here in ten minutes."

"Yeah, Norman." Brian smirked.

"**So** flipping unfair," muttered Norm.

"Language," said Dave.

"Shut up, Dave!"

"Muuuuum!" wailed Dave. "Norman just told me to shut up!"

"Yes, I **know** he did, Dave," said Norm's mum. "And it wasn't very nice of him. And by the way it's **not** unfair, Norman. We've **all** got things to do, you know. So hurry up. Because they'll be here in **nine** minutes now!"

Gordon flipping Bennet, thought Norm, reluctantly dragging himself off towards the utility room once again. Because no matter how much he **didn't** want his perfect cousins to come, he knew that they were **going** to. Nothing would stop them. Resistance was futile. If this were a movie, **they'd** be the monster. A great big three-headed monster. And it was just a matter of time before it came looming and lumbering over the horizon. And talking of time, thought Norm, if his mum said they'd be here in nine minutes? They flipping well **would** be here in nine minutes. Because not only were his cousins almost superhumanly perfect and annoying, they were also freakishly punctual.

Well at least Auntie Jem and Uncle Steve were, anyway. So much so that Norm was pretty sure that if it ever looked like they were going to be **early** for something, they'd wait round the corner in the car rather than turn up a fraction of a second too soon.

Not only that, thought Norm, but why all the flipping fuss and panic and rushing around all of a sudden? OK, so they might be **family** – but they weren't the **Royal** Family. No matter how much Auntie Jem would like to **think** they were. And anyway, if they really **were** royal then wouldn't that make **Norm** royal too? Because **his** mum and Uncle Steve were brother and sister, weren't they? And actually, **Grandpa** was his **mum's** dad – **and** Uncle Steve's dad. So surely that would make **Grandpa**, like, actual King, or something! If only, thought Norm. Because Grandpa would be the best king *ever*. And thinking about it, he quite fancied the idea of being dropped off at school in a horse-drawn carriage. Not to mention being abso-flipping-lutely *loaded* and having a really *massive* garage bursting with the most expensive mountain bikes that money could buy.

And not only *that*, thought Norm, but was there *anything* more pointless than flipping *recycling*? Because if so, he'd like to know what it was. Actually, thought Norm, on second thoughts he *wouldn't* like to know what it was. There was enough rubbish cluttering up his head to begin with, without even *more* being dumped in there. And *that* kind of rubbish definitely *couldn't* be recycled, unfortunately. But honestly, what was the big deal about sorting out a few bottles and a couple of empty Coco Pops packets? How exactly was *that* supposed to save the flipping planet, any more than his dad going round switching off lights and turning down the heating was supposed to? Because Norm just didn't *get* it. He never flipping *had* and he never flipping *would*. As far as *he* was concerned, recycling was a bit like a trip to IKEA. A complete and utter waste of time.

But before Norm could even close the utility room door behind him, the bell rang. Surely that wasn't them already, was it? thought Norm. That couldn't *possibly* have been nine minutes. No flipping way! All he'd done was walk here from the kitchen and then think some stuff. But not *that* much stuff. Certainly not nine *minutes'* worth of stuff.

The doorbell rang again. Seemingly no one *else* thought that it could be his aunt and uncle and cousins just yet, either.

"NORMAN?" yelled Norm's dad from the kitchen.

"WHAT?" yelled Norm.

"AREN'T YOU GOING TO ANSWER THE DOOR?"

"WHAAAAAAAAAAT?" yelled Norm again, but taking at least three times as long to yell it.

"YOU HEARD!" yelled his dad. "GO AND SEE WHO IT IS!"

"WHY SHOULD *I* DO IT, DAD?"

"I'M GOING TO PRETEND YOU DIDN'T *SAY* THAT, NORMAN!"

Norm sighed. His dad could flipping *pretend* all he liked, but he'd still flipping *said* it. And anyway, why *should* he go and see who was at the door? Why couldn't someone *else* do it?

"WE'RE BUSY, LOVE!" yelled Norm's mum as if she'd known exactly what Norm was thinking.

"SO AM I!" blurted Norm, **without** thinking.

"STOP YELLING!" yelled Norm's dad.

"BUT—"

"AND DON'T ANSWER BACK!"

Gordon flipping **Bennet**, thought Norm, trudging back out of the utility room, if anything even **more** slowly than he'd trudged into it in the **first** flipping place. Why did **he** have to do **everything** round here? Could things actually **be** more unfair?

CHAPTER 6

"Oh it's **you**, Norm," said Mikey, when Norm finally opened the front door.

Norm examined his best friend for a moment as if he was some kind of alien species he'd never actually clapped eyes on before. Not that Norm had ever clapped eyes on **any** kind of alien species before. Well, apart from his brothers. But that wasn't the point. The point **was**, why was Mikey looking at him as if he was totally naked?

"Who were you **expecting** it to be, Mikey? The flipping Easter Bunny?

Mikey pulled a face.

"I do actually **live** here, you doughnut," said Norm.

"What?" said Mikey. "Yeah, I know you do."

"Well, then."

"It's just that…"

"Just that what?" said Norm.

Mikey shrugged. "I dunno. I was just expecting someone **else** to open the door, that's all."

Norm sighed. "Yeah, well. So was I."

"What?" said Mikey.

"I was expecting someone else to open it, as well," said Norm.

67

Mikey pulled a face. "So...why **didn't** someone else open it?"

"Because everyone **else** was too **'busy'**, apparently," said Norm, making quotation marks in the air with his fingers. "So **I** had to flipping do it. It's **SO** unfair."

Mikey nodded sympathetically. "I hear what you're saying."

Good, thought Norm. Because if Mikey **couldn't** hear what he was saying, there wasn't much flipping point **saying** it.

"You're all wet by the way," said Mikey."

"What?" said Norm.

"You're all wet."

"**Really?**" said Norm. "Thanks for pointing that out, Mikey. Because I'd never have flipping **known** otherwise."

"All right, all right," said Mikey. "No need to be so **sarcastic**, Norm."

"Flipping well **is**," said Norm.

Mikey knew better than to argue when Norm was in a mood like this. And Norm had been in a mood like this pretty much ever since they'd both been babies.

"And anyway, you're wet too, Mikey."

"Yeah, I know, but..."

"But what?"

Mikey shrugged again. "It's raining."

"Yeah? So?" said Norm.

"Erm, you're inside," said Mikey.

"Gordon flipping **Bennet**!" said Norm. "You think I don't **know** that? What do you take me for, Mikey? Some kind of **idiot**?"

"**No!**" protested Mikey. "**Course** not, Norm!"

"So?"

"So have you just stepped out of the shower, or something?"

"Seriously?" said Norm.

Mikey nodded.

"OK," said Norm. "Well firstly it's none of your flipping **business**, Mikey. And secondly, we don't actually **have** a flipping shower in this house."

"Oh, yeah," said Mikey sheepishly. "Sorry, Norm. I forgot."

Norm glared at Mikey, like an owl sizing up a mouse. Even though he knew perfectly well that it wasn't **Mikey's** fault they'd moved house. Or rather, it wasn't Mikey's fault that they'd **had** to move house. And even though he knew it wasn't **Mikey's** fault that compared to Norm, he lived a life of complete and utter luxury. Then again, thought Norm, there were probably tribes of llama farmers in Papua New Guinea Pig, or wherever, who were living more luxurious lives than **he** was. Not that

that was Mikey's fault either. But it still hurt. And every time Norm was reminded of just how rubbish things had become since his dad had lost his job, it  felt like a kick in the teeth. Yeah, thought Norm. And as far as he was concerned, there'd been a few too many kicks in the teeth just lately. Much more of this and he was going to have to start liquidising all his meals and drinking them through a flipping straw. Because at this rate he wasn't going to have enough teeth left to chew with!

"So?" said Mikey expectantly.

"Are you ready?"

"Ready for **what**?" said Norm.

Mikey looked at Norm as if he couldn't quite make up his mind whether he was joking or not. Surely Norm knew what **day** it was, didn't he? And surely he knew what they both usually **did** on that day, didn't he? If not, then something was **seriously** wrong. Either Norm was ill, or he'd been abducted by extra-terrestrials and this was actually a cloned **version** of Norm that he was talking to. Because—

"What are you looking at me like that for?" said Norm.

"Erm," began Mikey hesitantly. "Have you **forgotten**, Norm?"

"Have I forgotten **what**?" said Norm.

"That we're meant to be going **biking**?"

"**Biking?**" said Norm, as if this had been literally the furthest thing from his mind. As if biking wasn't the single most important thing in his life. As if he didn't think about it night and day. At least, the bits of night and day when he was actually **awake**. And as if, when he **wasn't** actually awake he wasn't **dreaming** about biking, instead.

"Yeah," said Mikey. "It's Saturday."

Norm exhaled like a leaky lilo. What with everything else going on in his head, the unthinkable had happened. He'd actually **forgotten** that he was supposed to be going biking with Mikey. And Norm had never **ever** forgotten **that** before, in all the years since he and Mikey had finally dispensed with their stabilisers and been able to balance on two wheels instead of four. He'd forgotten plenty of **other** things

since then. Unimportant, **_trivial_** things that really didn't matter, like where the toilet in his new house was and whether or not he'd got any homework. But forgetting about going **_biking_**? There was more chance of Norm forgetting to eat, breathe or sleep.

"Well?" said Mikey.

"I can't," said Norm, somehow unable to look Mikey directly in the eye and staring at the ground instead.

"You can't go **_biking_**?" said Mikey. "**_Seriously?_**"

Norm suddenly looked up and glared at Mikey so witheringly that for a moment or two, Mikey was genuinely quite scared.

"How long have we known each other, Mikey?"

"A very long time," said Mikey.

"Correct," said Norm. "And **_in_** that very long time, have I **_ever_** joked about not being able to go **_biking_**?"

Mikey thought for a moment. "No, Norm. I don't think you have."

"Exactly," said Norm. "Because there are **some** things it's not OK to joke about. And **biking's** one of them."

Mikey waited for a couple of seconds, to make absolutely sure that Norm had finished saying whatever he was going to say. And it appeared that he had.

"Why, Norm?"

Norm pulled a face, as if this was the most ridiculous question he'd ever heard. Which, up to **that** point in his life, it **was**. "**Why?**"

Mikey nodded.

"Why is it not OK to joke about **biking?**"

"What?" said Mikey. "No! I meant **why** can't you come biking, Norm?"

"Oh, right," said Norm. "How long have you got?"

Mikey shrugged. "All day, if we're not going biking."

Norm looked at Mikey for a second. Had he really just said what he *thought* he'd just said? "Pardon?"

"I said all day, if we're not going biking."

"*We're?*" said Norm.

Mikey nodded.

"You mean…"

"What?" said Mikey.

"*You* won't go biking if *I* can't?"

"Course I won't," said Mikey. "How *could* I? It's a complete no-brainer, Norm."

Norm suddenly felt guilty for being grumpy with Mikey earlier on. In fact, not just earlier on, but ever. Because if it had been the other way round and Mikey had been the one who couldn't go biking?

He'd have been off down the road like a flipping shot. He wouldn't even have given it a second thought. And even if he **had** given it a second thought, it wouldn't have made the slightest bit of difference. He'd have **still** been off down the road like a flipping shot. How could Mikey **possibly** be so nice? It was enough to make you sick, thought Norm. Well, enough to make **him** sick, anyway.

"Aw, that's a pity," said Mikey, looking skywards.

"Uh?" said Norm. "What is?"

"It's stopped **raining**."

Mikey was right, thought Norm, looking skywards, too. It **had** stopped raining. Which somehow made it even **more** annoying that he couldn't go biking today. With **or** without Mikey. And it was already completely off the scale on the annoying-ometer. Or at least it **would** have been if there was actually such a **thing** as an annoying-ometer. Which there wasn't. Which was pretty annoying in **itself**. But that wasn't the point, thought Norm. The point was, he was suddenly so consumed with a mixture of frustration and irritation and sheer unadulterated **rage**, he felt like he was going to erupt at any moment.

"Well?" said Mikey.

"Well what?" said Norm.

"Why not?" said Mikey.

"Why not **what?**" said Norm.

"**Why** can't you go **biking**?" said Mikey.

"**That's** why not," said Norm, looking over Mikey's shoulder as a car pulled up directly outside the house and tooted its horn several times.

"What do you mean?" said Mikey.

"I mean I can't go flipping biking because my perfect flipping cousins have just arrived, haven't they?"

"Oh, I see," said Mikey, turning round. "Bad luck, Norm."

Bad luck? thought Norm. Mikey wasn't kidding! It was abso-flipping-lutely **disastrous** luck! Even worse than the time he did a particularly stinky fart in a department store lift, just before the doors opened and his head teacher got in.

"Cooool!" said Mikey.

"What is?" said Norm.

"The *car*," said Mikey.

Great, thought Norm. That was *all* he flipping needed. Mikey being impressed by his perfect flipping cousins' car. Well, Uncle Steve and Auntie Jem's car, anyway. But honestly. Talk about rubbing salt in the wound, or whatever that expression was. Just when he thought he couldn't feel any *more* hard done by and lousier than he already *did?* Because Norm didn't know too much about cars. But he knew enough to know that if *Mikey* was impressed, it *must* be a really cool one. Because Mikey's parents had a pretty flash car *themselves*.

And to think, thought Norm, only a couple of minutes ago he'd actually been feeling **bad** that he'd snapped at Mikey. Now he was secretly quite **glad**. Served him flipping right! The traitor. Well, maybe he wasn't a **traitor**. But—

"COOOO-EEEEEEE! NOOOOOR-MAN!" yelled Auntie Jem as she got out of the car and before Norm had the chance to finish thinking what he'd been thinking.

Gordon flipping **Bennet**, thought Norm. Why did she have to go and do **that**? Shriek like a demented donkey, so that everyone within a five hundred metre radius could hear her? He thought his **brothers** were loud. But honestly, Auntie Jem made Brian and Dave seem like a couple of mice with tonsillitis, by comparison. She was like a flipping **foghorn**. Everything she ever said she said at maximum volume. As if she

was addressing thousands of people at some kind of demonstration and speaking through a flipping loudhailer. Not that Auntie Jem would actually **need** a loudhailer, of course. But that wasn't the point, thought Norm. The point was, why couldn't she just have waved, or waited till she'd got a bit closer before saying anything? Like a **normal** person would have done? But **oh no**. She just had to make a great big song and dance of it, didn't she? Just like she had to make a great big song and dance about **everything**. Unlike Uncle Steve, who was the complete and utter opposite. How he and Auntie Jem ever went out with each other in the first place – let alone ended up actually **marrying** each other – was the eighth wonder of the world, as far as Norm was concerned. Not that he knew what the other seven were. Or cared, for that matter. All Norm cared about at that precise moment was the fact that his three perfect cousins had, by now, also got out of the car and were making their way towards him, grinning their stupid, perfect heads off.

"Hi, Norman," said Danny, Norm's youngest perfect cousin.

"Hi, Norman," said Becky, Norm's **next** youngest perfect cousin. Or second **oldest** perfect cousin, depending on which way he looked at it.

"Hi, Norman," said Ed, Norm's oldest perfect cousin, **whichever** way he flipping looked at it.

"All right?" mumbled Norm, starting as he meant to carry on, firstly by talking to all three at once wherever possible and secondly by saying no more to them than was strictly necessary.

"We're good," said Danny.

"We're cool," said Becky.

"We're cool and good," said Ed.

And that was all it took. Just eight little words – two each from Danny and Becky, plus four from Ed – to remind Norm just **how** annoying his perfect flipping cousins **could** be. In fact, never mind could be. **Were**. Permanently. Not that Norm actually

needed reminding, of course. It wasn't as if it had temporarily slipped his mind, like so many other things tended to do. As far as **he** was concerned, Danny, Becky and Ed were never ever **not** annoying. But even by **their** standards, it hadn't taken long to wind him up like an overwound clock.

"You're Mickey, right?" said Ed, turning to Mikey.

"Er, it's **Mikey**, actually," said Mikey.

"Same thing," said Ed. "Mickey. Mikey. Whatever."

Norm could feel the anger gradually beginning to bubble away inside. Or it could just have been a bit of wind. Either way he was going to have to release it sooner or later.

"Just ignore him, Mikey," said Becky, grinning. "He's an idiot."

"What?" Ed laughed.

"Well it's true," said Becky. "You *are*."

Ed thought for a second. "Yeah, fair enough."

"Now apologise," said Becky.

"What?" said Ed. "Oh right, yeah. Sorry, Mikey. I was just..."

"Being an idiot," said Becky.

Ed shrugged. "Yeah. What *she* said."

"Honestly, it's fine," said Mikey.

Norm gawped at Mikey like a hypnotised goldfish. What on earth was he *on* about? It wasn't *fine*. It was the complete flipping *opposite* of fine. Whatever that was. Unfine? Who cared? That wasn't the point. The point was, how would *Ed* like it if someone got *his* stupid name wrong?

Deliberately!

"So we're cool?" said Ed.

"Yeah, we're cool," said Mikey, nodding.

"Put it there, bro'," said Ed, holding his hand out for Mikey to shake.

No, Mikey, thought Norm. **Don't** put it there! Put it anywhere **but** there. Don't be tricked into thinking they're **nice**. Because that was clearly all part of their cunning plan. To suck you in and fool you into believing that they were vaguely **human**. But it was already too late. Mikey **had** put it there. And worse still, once they'd shaken hands, Mikey and Ed even bumped fists, like they were flipping rappers, or skateboarders or something. Which **definitely** wasn't on, as far as Norm was concerned. Because even **he** and Mikey didn't bump fists. And he and Mikey had been best friends forever! Well, not **forever**, obviously. But since they'd been in nappies, anyway. And another thing, thought Norm. What kind of doughnut called anyone **bro'**, for goodness' sake? An abso-flipping-lutely **massive** doughnut. That was what kind.

"Awesome," said Danny.

Uh? thought Norm. **What** was awesome? Nothing, as far as he could see. And how come **Mikey** wasn't getting wound up by Norm's cousins, too?

Surely **he** found them just as annoying as Norm did, didn't he? Didn't **everyone?** Unless **that** was all part of their cunning plan, too? To annoy **Norm** and Norm alone? Thinking about it, thought Norm, thinking about it, that was probably **exactly** what their cunning plan was. Because Mikey didn't seem in the **least** bit bothered by them. And if he **was** then he was a flipping good actor.

"Hi, guys," said Uncle Steve, wandering up the drive with Auntie Jem.

"Hi," mumbled Norm.

"Hi," said Mikey.

"It's Mikey, isn't it?" said Uncle Steve.

Mikey nodded. "Yeah."

"How are you?"

"Fine thanks," said Mikey.

"Awesome," said Uncle Steve.

89

Gordon flipping **Bennet**, thought Norm. What was awesome about **that**?

"Have you just got out of the shower, Norman?" said Auntie Jem.

"What?" said Norm. "I mean, pardon?"

"You're all wet," said Auntie Jem. "Have you just got out of the shower?"

"Er, no," said Norm, glancing at Mikey. "I was just getting the washing in."

"Whoa," said Danny as if Norm had just announced that he'd been a dinosaur in a previous life. "You really have to do that?"

"Anyway, Mum," said Ed, "they don't actually **have** a shower. Remember?"

"Oh, of **course**!" said Auntie Jem. "I was forgetting. Not **all** houses have en suite bathrooms!"

"Muuuum!" hissed Becky.

"What?" said Auntie Jem innocently. "Was that a bit insensitive of me? I'm sorry."

Norm sighed. Were they doing this on purpose? Had they made some kind of bet, before they arrived? To see how quickly they could make him snap? Because at this flipping rate they wouldn't have long to wait.

"Well I suppose I'd better be off then," said Mikey, turning to leave.

"But..." began Norm.

"I'll see you later, Norm."

Norm watched enviously as his best friend climbed onto his bike and began pedalling down the drive. How he wished that **he** could do the same, instead of being cooped up with his stupid, infuriatingly perfect cousins. It wasn't just **unfair**. It was positively **inhumane**.

"See you later, Mickey!" yelled Ed.

"It's **Mikey**, you idiot!" said Becky.

"See you later, Mikey, you idiot!" yelled Ed.

"Ed!" said Uncle Steve sternly.

"Hey, chillax, Dad!" said Ed. "It was just a *joke*."

"Ha! Good one, bro'!" Danny laughed.

Norm closed his eyes for a few moments. But when he opened them again, nothing had changed. Everything was exactly the same. It *hadn't* all been a dream, as he'd been hoping. Worse flipping luck.

"Are you going to ask us in, then, Norman?" said Uncle Steve. "Or are we going to have to stand out here all day?"

"Oh right, yeah. Sorry. Come in," said Norm.

"Awesome," said Uncle Steve, stepping into the house.

Norm took a deep breath before slowly letting it out again. Because if he hadn't, he might well have exploded.

CHAPTER 7

Any faint, lingering hope Norm might have had that the worst was over and that the rest of his day might actually get just a **teensy** bit better, was soon **snuffed** out. In fact, never mind snuffed out, any faint, lingering hope he might have had was shredded, run over by a ten tonne truck and finally fed to a school of ravenous piranhas. Not

that Norm had ever **truly** thought that there was any **real** possibility of the day getting any better. Even just a **teensy** bit better. In his experience, the worst was very rarely over. There was nearly always something even **more** rubbish or **more** unfair lurking just around the corner. Life for Norm wasn't so much a series of peaks and troughs as a series of troughs followed by even more troughs.

"Ah, there you are," said Norm's dad when Norm eventually walked into the kitchen a few minutes later, having taken as long as possible to change into some dry clothes and thereby avoid being in his cousins' company for as long as possible.

"We thought you'd got **lost**, love!" Norm's mum laughed.

No such flipping luck, thought Norm.

"It would be easy to get lost in **our** house, because it's so big!" said Danny.

Yeah, whatever, thought Norm. It would be easy to get lost in Danny's **head**, because that was so flipping big, too.

"Have you washed your hands?" asked his dad.

"Yeah," said Norm, sitting down at the table. Or rather, sitting down at the two tables pushed together.

"I mean recently, Norman. Not have you **ever** washed them?"

"That's very funny, Dad," said Dave.

"We've washed **our** hands!" said Danny. "Haven't we, guys?"

"Totally!" chirruped Becky and Ed together.

"Awesome," said Uncle Steve.

Gordon flipping **Bennet**, thought Norm. Could they not give it a rest? Just for a couple of minutes? Even a couple of **seconds**. And anyway, he didn't actually **need** to wash his hands, did he? He'd just had an all-over wash in the flipping garden!

"Mmmm," said Uncle Steve as Norm's mum plonked down a big serving dish in front of him and removed the lid. "Something smells good!"

"Oh, it's nothing," said Norm's mum, modestly.

"My **favourite**!" said Brian.

Uh? thought Norm. Brian's favourite was **nothing**? He'd always known his middle brother was **weird**. But he had no idea he was **that** weird.

"Lasagne?" said Dave. "Yum, yum, my bum!"

"***Dave!***" said Norm's dad.

"What?" said Dave.

"Language!"

"Sorry," said Dave, trying not to giggle.

"Is it homemade, Auntie Linda?" said Becky.

"Sorry?" said Norm's mum.

"I was just wondering if you made the lasagne yourself?"

Norm's mum hesitated. "Erm, not exactly."

"Not exactly?"

"No. I didn't."

"Oh, that's a shame," said Auntie Jem.

"I know," said Norm's mum apologetically. "I'm afraid I just didn't have time."

"We all have *time*, Linda," said Auntie Jem. "It's just a question of how we choose to *use* it."

"I was working, actually," said Norm's mum.

"*Working?*" said Auntie Jem, aghast.

"Yes," said Norm's mum, nodding. "At the cake shop."

"Poor thing," said Auntie Jem. "How *awful* for you."

What was *that* supposed to mean? wondered Norm. That it was awful his mum had to *work*? Or that it was awful she had to work at a cake shop? One thing was for sure. He doubted it was very complimentary.

"Anyway," said Uncle Steve, "it's very nice of you to ask us over, Linda. And I'm sure the lasagne will be delicious, whether it's homemade or not."

Norm's mum smiled gratefully at her brother.

"Thank you, Steven."

"As long as it's vegetarian," said Auntie Jem.

Time appeared to stop for a few moments. Everything went very quiet.

"Sorry, what was that?" said Norm's mum.

"Oh, nothing." Auntie Jem smiled. "I just said as long as it's vegetarian. That's all."

That's all? thought Norm. That's **all?** Auntie Jem might as well have said 'as long as it's completely tasteless and has about as much nutritional value as a pair of grilled slippers'. Because as far as **Norm** was concerned, vegetarian food wasn't actually food at all. Not **proper** food anyway. Even though strictly speaking, Margherita pizza was actually vegetarian.

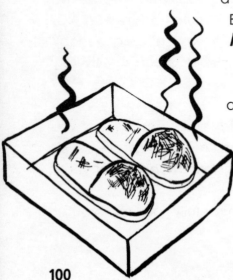

And Margherita pizza was most definitely **Norm's** favourite. But somehow that was different.

"Erm…" began Norm's mum hesitantly.

"What is it, Linda?" said Auntie Jem.

"Have you…"

"Have I, **what?**"

"Gone…vegetarian?" said Norm's mum.

"Oh, **sorry!**" said Auntie Jem. "Didn't we tell you?"

"**We?**" said Norm's mum.

Auntie Jem nodded.

"Have you **all** gone vegetarian?"

"Well, of course," said Auntie Jem. "Makes life **so** much easier!"

"Since when?"

"Since yesterday actually."

"**Yesterday?**" said Norm's mum incredulously. "You might have…"

"Might have **what**?" said Auntie Jem.

Norm's mum sighed. "Nothing."

"I take it it's **not** vegetarian, then," said Auntie Jem. "That's a pity."

A pity? thought Norm. Not for him personally, it wasn't. Because at least it meant he could have a really **massive** portion of lasagne. But did Auntie Jem really have to be quite so flipping rude and blunt about it? How was his mum supposed to know they'd gone flipping vegetarian yesterday? She wasn't flipping **psychic**, was she? Had it been on the news? Had it...

Norm suddenly stopped mid-thought. Was he actually **defending** his mum and sticking up for her? Maybe not out loud. But in his head? He **was**, wasn't he? What on earth had come over him? Was he ill? Was he in the grip of some strange mysterious force? Or was he, at the ripe old age of nearly thirteen, finally beginning to grow up? Well, whatever it was, it felt most peculiar, thought Norm. He might have to go and have a lie down.

"Does that mean you're not going to eat it, Jemma?" said Norm's mum.

"I'm sorry but we **can't** eat it, Linda," said Auntie Jem. "On principle."

Norm's dad pulled a face. "A principle you only decided you had **yesterday**?"

"Alan," said Auntie Jem, as if she was talking to one of Norm's **brothers** and not his **dad**. As if she couldn't quite believe that she was actually having to **explain** this to an **adult**. "I – er, I mean **we** – didn't only **decide yesterday**."

"Oh, really?" said Norm's dad, clearly not convinced.

"Yes, **really**," said Auntie Jem. "It's been more of a...**gradual** realisation."

"And you all **gradually** realised at the **same** time, did you?" said Norm's dad, clearly **still** not convinced.

"It's like, totally not cool to eat animals," said Ed.

Norm's dad pulled a face. "But it was OK to eat them the day *before* yesterday?"

"We mustn't *preach*, Ed," said Becky. "We must respect other people's views."

"Yeah," said Danny. "Even if they're wrong."

Norm had occasionally heard people say that 'you could cut the tension with a knife'. But he'd never really known what it meant, before. Why should he? It was just some boring expression that grown-ups came out with from time to time, along with a million *other* boring expressions. But now, as Norm waited for Auntie Jem's next response, he knew *exactly* what it meant. It meant that things were about to kick off.

Norm's mum sighed again. "Well, I'm very sorry but I just don't know what to..."

"It's OK, Auntie Linda," said Becky. "We can just have salad instead."

Salad? thought Norm. Who in their right flipping mind would ever willingly 'just have' salad instead? Without actually being **forced** to have it? Apart from maybe a rabbit? And even then it would have to be a pretty **desperate** rabbit, as far as **Norm** was concerned. Then again, each to their own and all that. People could eat whatever they **wanted** to eat. It was just that, well, anyone who voluntarily ate salad was just plain weird, thought Norm. And **wrong**.

"You do **have** salad, right?" said Becky.

"Salad?" said Norm's mum. "Yes, there's a bag in the fridge."

Everything went very quiet again. But not for long.

"Did you say a **bag** of salad, Linda?" said Auntie Jem.

"Yes. Why?" said Norm's mum.

Yes, **why**? thought Norm. What did it matter if the salad came in a **bag** or in the back of a flipping **taxi**? The point was it was still flipping **salad** – and therefore evil and to be avoided at all costs.

"Well, for one thing," said Auntie Jem, "if you grow your **own** salad—"

"Like **we** do," Danny interjected.

"That's right, Danny," said Auntie Jem. "Like **we** do…"

Of **course**, thought Norm. Like **they** flipping did. Although knowing **them**, they probably had a flipping **gardener** to do the actual **growing** bit **for** them.

"Seriously," said Ed. "You'd be amazed at the variety of lettuces you can get these days."

Seriously? thought Norm. He flipping well **wouldn't**. He couldn't care **less** about the variety of flipping lettuces you could get these days. That had to be one of the most **boring** sentences he'd ever heard in his life. And Norm had heard some pretty boring sentences in his time. Most of them spoken by either his mum or his dad. But the **worrying** thing was, Ed wasn't all that much older than **he** was. What on **earth** was he doing banging on about flipping **lettuces**? Seriously. He needed to get out more.

"Indeed, Ed," said Auntie Jem. "But as I was saying, if you grow your **own** salad, not only is it healthier and **better** for you, but..."

"But what?" said Norm's dad.

"Well, if you don't mind me saying," said Auntie Jem.

"Saying **what**, Jemma?" said Norm's dad, the vein on the side of his head just beginning to throb. Not that Norm noticed, of course. He was far more interested to know what Auntie Jem **was** about to come out with than he was with whether his dad was getting stressed or not. Because whatever Auntie Jem was about to come out with, Norm was pretty flipping sure that he **would** mind her saying it.

"It's also a lot **cheaper**."

"Pardon?" said Norm's dad.

Auntie Jem shrugged. "It's a lot cheaper. It could actually save you money."

Norm's dad eyeballed Auntie Jem for a few seconds before speaking, very slowly and very deliberately. "What's your point, Jemma?"

"Oh, I don't think we need to go into this just now, do you?" said Norm's mum, intervening.

"Oh, but I think we do," said Norm's dad, still staring at Auntie Jem.

"I just think that under the circumstances..." began Auntie Jem.

"And what circumstances are **they**?"

"Well, you know…" said Auntie Jem.

"No, I **don't** know actually, Jemma," said Norm's dad. "Why don't you tell me?"

Norm could feel himself getting angrier and angrier. Because he was pretty sure he knew **exactly** what circumstances Auntie Jem was talking about. What little patience he'd had in the first place was rapidly draining away like water from a bathtub. His fuse was getting shorter and shorter. He couldn't bite his tongue much longer. Any second now and he was going to go off like a flipping rocket. It didn't matter which one of them said anything. He'd had enough.

"Mum says you're skint," said Danny matter-of-factly. "That's why everything you eat is supermarket own-brand."

"SHUT UP!" yelled Norm at the top of his lungs. "JUST FLIPPING WELL SHUT UP!"

All of a sudden, everything went **really** quiet. Never mind quiet enough to hear a pin drop. It was quiet enough to hear a pin drop in the house next door.

"Apologise," said Norm's mum, eventually breaking the silence.

Yeah, thought Norm. Flipping apologise, Danny. Not only for **that**, but for everything else, too. And then flipping **go**. And don't come back. Because...

Hang on, thought Norm, suddenly jamming on his mental brakes. Why wasn't anyone saying anything? And more worryingly, why was everybody looking at **him**?

"Well, Norman?" said Norm's mum.

Norm pulled a face. "Well what?"

"What do you mean, well what?" said his mum. "**Apologise!**"

"Uh?" said Norm. "**Me?**"

"Yes, **you**."

"Apologise?"

"Well, of course," said Norm's mum.

"But..."

"What?"

"It should be **them** who have to apologise, Mum! Not **me**!"

"I'll give you one more chance," said Norm's mum.

Norm sighed. Where was the flipping justice?

Because as far as **he** could see, there **wasn't** any justice! What was he **supposed** to have done? Just sat there like a flipping **doughnut** and allowed them to say whatever they wanted? No flipping **way!** His only regret was that he hadn't said it sooner.

"Well?" said Norm's mum. "I'm waiting."

"THAT IS **SO** UNFAIR!" bawled Norm.

"Oh, you **think** so?" said his mum.

"I flipping know so," said Norm.

"Right, that's it! Out!"

"What?" said Norm.

"You heard," said Norm's mum, pointing towards the door. "Out! **Now!**"

Norm didn't need telling a third time. He was off his seat and halfway up the stairs before you could say 'abso-flipping-lutely!'

CHAPTER 8

It was only when Norm **was** halfway up the stairs
that it suddenly occurred to him. Fair enough. So
his mum had told him to get **out**. But what she
hadn't told him was where he should get out **of**.
Out of the room? Or out of the house
altogether? It was the sort of
comment that was open to
a certain amount of...what
was the word? wondered
Norm.   Interpretation?
Yeah, interpretation. That
was it. And the way that
Norm chose to interpret
it was that, as his mum
hadn't specified that he
should go to his **room** –
as she probably **meant**
to – he could go wherever

he **wanted** to go. Well, not **literally** wherever he wanted. He couldn't just jump in a cab, head for the airport and get on the first available flight out of the country. Who knows **where** he might have ended up? But what he **could** do was jump on his **bike** and go for a ride.

As he pedalled off down the street, Norm couldn't help chuckling to himself. Not too loudly, of course, in case anyone heard him and told him to get back to the house. But honestly, did his mum **really** think that was supposed to be a **punishment**? To make him get up and leave the table – and **not** have to look at his perfect cousins' stupid grinning faces any more? **Not** have to put up with their never-ending smugness and their all-round flipping annoyingness any more? Not have to listen to Auntie Jem's snarky comments and thinly veiled criticisms any more? Because that wasn't a **punishment**, as far as Norm was concerned. A **punishment** would have been to make him **stay** at the flipping table and have to put up with them for even **longer**! No, thought Norm. Telling him to get out was more like a flipping **treat**!

How did **Uncle Steve** put up with it? That's what **Norm** wanted to know. Did he possess some kind of superhuman powers? He **must** do. Either that or he was officially the nicest human being **ever**. It had to be one or the other, thought Norm. How else could you explain it? Because it was bad enough having to live under the same roof as his flipping **brothers**. But by comparison, his perfect cousins made Brian and Dave seem almost…well, almost **nice**. Unless Uncle Steve had just got **used** to them and didn't actually **notice** how annoying they were. Perhaps they genuinely didn't bother him any more. Maybe he'd become immune to them. Like cows eventually became immune to buzzing flies. It seemed unlikely, though, thought Norm. Because he'd **never** get used to his perfect flipping cousins. Not in a million flipping years. It just wasn't **ever** going to happen.

"Earth to Norman. Come in please, Norman," said a disembodied voice from a galaxy far, far away. At least it **seemed** like a disembodied voice, to

Norm. But it wasn't really. It was just Grandpa. And he wasn't actually in a galaxy far, far away, at all. He was in the allotments.

"Over here, you numpty!"

"Uh? What?" said Norm, skidding to a halt before turning around and finally seeing Grandpa staring at him from the other side of the wire mesh fence. "Oh, hi, Grandpa. Didn't realise where I was."

"Pardon?" said Grandpa.

"I didn't realise where I was," said Norm.

Grandpa frowned, until his cloud-like eyebrows met in the middle and formed one big cloud. "How can you not realise where you *are*?"

Norm shrugged. "Dunno. Just didn't."

Grandpa examined Norm for a few seconds, as if he was studying a rare work of art.

"Where are you going?"

"What?" said Norm.

"Where are you going?" said Grandpa again.

Norm shrugged again. "Nowhere at the moment."

Grandpa sighed. "I mean where **were** you going, before you **stopped**?"

"Oh, right," said Norm. "Dunno, really."

Grandpa frowned again. Not that he'd ever really stopped. "You don't **know?**"

"Not really, no," said Norm.

"You must have **some** idea, Norman. Surely."

"Nah," said Norm. "I was just…"

"Just what?" said Grandpa.

"Dunno," said Norm. "I was just…"

"In a world of your own?"

Norm thought for a moment. That's exactly where he'd been, just now. A world of his own. And if it hadn't been for Grandpa spotting him and calling out he probably still **would** be.

"A penny for them?" said Grandpa.

"Uh?" said Norm.

"A penny for your **thoughts**?"

Gordon flipping **Bennet**, thought Norm. A **penny** for your thoughts might have seemed like a lot of money when **Grandpa** was a boy. But that was about six hundred years ago. You could have probably bought a flipping **car** for a penny six hundred years ago. Well, if cars had actually been **invented** six hundred years ago, you could.

But that wasn't the point, thought Norm. The point was he wasn't going to suddenly start divulging his innermost secrets for a flipping **penny**. Not even to **Grandpa**. And he'd **normally** talk to Grandpa about pretty much **anything**. For **free**. And anyway, what could he actually **say**? That he couldn't **stand** his cousins? That every little thing about them irritated him and made him want to vomit up his internal organs? That if he never saw them again, it would be too soon? No. He couldn't very well say **that**, could he? Because, unbe-flipping-lievably, not only was Grandpa his grandpa – and Brian and Dave's grandpa, too – Grandpa was **also** Danny and Becky and Ed's grandpa, as well! How was that even **possible**? wondered Norm. You know – apart from the whole biological-**relation** thing? Because the more Norm thought about it, the more unlikely and incredible it seemed. Practically the only thing they had in common, as far as Norm could see, was that they all had heads. Apart from that? Nothing.

"Well?" said Grandpa. "Deal or no deal?"

"No deal," mumbled Norm.

"Hmmm," said Grandpa, examining Norm again. "In that case, how about something to eat?"

"What?" said Norm.

"Well, you must be pretty hungry."

Norm thought for a moment. He *was* pretty hungry actually. Hardly surprising either, since he'd left the house without having had so much as a mouthful of lasagne. But how would Grandpa have known *that*?

"I can read you like a book, Norman."

Uh? thought Norm. What had flipping

books got to do with anything? Books were made up and stupid and full of things that could never actually happen in real life, like dragons and wizards and stuff. Now, if there was a book about a kid who was into mountain biking? That would be a **different** story, thought Norm. One that he **might** actually flipping **read**.

"Tell me about it," said Grandpa.

"Tell you about **what**?" said Norm.

"Don't play dumb," said Grandpa. "You know perfectly well what I mean."

Do I? thought Norm. In that case he wished Grandpa would hurry up and flipping well say what it was.

"I know what they can be like."

Norm pulled a face. "Who?"

"Your **cousins**," said Grandpa.

Norm stared at Grandpa as if Grandpa had just pulled off the most amazing magical illusion ever.

"How did you **know**, Grandpa?"

"Oh, I know **everything**," said Grandpa, his eyes crinkling just a little bit in the corners. Which was the closest that Grandpa ever got to smiling.

"Really?" said Norm.

"No, not really, you numpty," said Grandpa. "I was invited for lunch, too."

Norm breathed a sigh of relief. Much as he loved Grandpa, the thought of him actually knowing **everything** was just a little bit creepy.

"Well?" said Grandpa.

"Well what?" said Norm.

"Ask me why I didn't go," said Grandpa.

"What?" said Norm. "Oh, right. Erm, so why didn't you go, Grandpa?"

"Funny you should ask," said Grandpa.

"No it's not," said Norm. "You just told me to."

"Because I know what they can be *like*."

"Uh?" said Norm.

"***That's*** why I didn't ***go***," said Grandpa. "To ***lunch***. At your house. Because I know what they can be ***like***. So I said I was too busy. Come on, Norman. Keep up."

Gordon flipping ***Bennet***, thought Norm. He was ***trying*** to keep up. But it wasn't easy sometimes. And right now was one of those sometimes.

"Let's face it. They can be a little bit..."

Grandpa paused. As if he was weighing up which word to use. As if he too was suddenly aware that not only was he Norm and Brian and Dave's grandpa, he was Danny and Becky and Ed's grandpa, too.

"Challenging?" said Norm, remembering what his mum had said earlier.

"Yes, that's **one** way of putting it, I suppose," said Grandpa. "I can think of several others. They're very…"

"Competitive?" said Norm.

"Yes," said Grandpa. "Competitive. Good word. You're on a roll, Norman."

Norm secretly felt quite pleased with himself. It wasn't every day he thought of a big word. Let alone **two** big words.

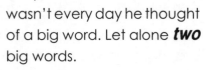

"And I'm not saying that's necessarily a **bad** thing, by the way," said Grandpa. "Being competitive can be a very **good** thing, sometimes."

Norm nodded again.

"I mean you're never going to become World Thingy Doo-dah – whatever it is you want to become – without being **competitive**, are you?"

"World Mountain Biking Champion?" said Norm.

"That's the one," said Grandpa. "But there's a time and a place for everything, Norman. Would you agree?"

"Definitely," said Norm, even though he wasn't a hundred per cent sure what Grandpa was talking about any more. But he got the gist. And the gist seemed to be that Grandpa had also been invited for lunch, but had chosen not to go because he thought his cousins were annoying, too. Well, his **grandchildren**. Well, not **all** his grandchildren. But Danny, Becky and Ed.

"I'm just not a big fan of family gatherings," said Grandpa. "I know I'm probably not supposed to say that. But it's the truth. It's how I feel. It's all just noise after a while. It can all get a bit much."

Yes, thought Norm. It flipping well **could** get a bit much. And it flipping well just **had** got a bit much. Not for the first time, Grandpa had hit the nail firmly and squarely on the head.

"Two's company, three's a crowd and all that."

"What?" said Norm.

"It's just an expression," said Grandpa.

Norm smiled. There was nothing **quite** like a dose of Grandpa to cheer him up when he was feeling a bit down in the dumps. The effect was almost instantaneous. Like a breath of fresh air after being stuck in a fart-filled lift. Because Grandpa said what he thought. And what he thought, made **sense**. He never tried to jazz it up, or deliberately use loads of fancy words, like **most** grown-ups did. He spoke in a language Norm could actually **understand**. Well, apart from the odd expression here and there. But apart from **that**, Norm could understand it. And not only that but Norm truly believed that Grandpa understood **him**, too – and that they shared some kind of special **bond**. Just the two of them. A bond which went much, much deeper than mere language. Not that grandparents were allowed to have **favourites**, of course. But if they did...

"Earth to Norman," said Grandpa.

"What?" said Norm.

"You were miles away again, weren't you?"

"Yeah," said Norm.

"So?"

"What?" said Norm.

"You hungry?"

Norm grinned. "Yeah, I am. **Really** hungry."

"Aw, that's a pity," said Grandpa.

"Why's that?" said Norm.

"Because I haven't got anything to eat here."

"Seriously, Grandpa?"

"Seriously," said Grandpa, his eyes crinkling in the corners again. Not that Norm noticed. And not that he found it very funny either, Grandpa leading him on like that. As if he was suddenly going to produce something enticing for him to eat. "Unless…"

"Yeah?" said Norm, brightening a little.

"You like lettuce?" said Grandpa, turning round and gesturing towards his allotment with a dramatic sweep of an arm.

Gordon flipping **Bennet**, thought Norm. Why was everyone so obsessed with flipping **lettuce** today? Or **any** day, for that matter! Because frankly, he'd sooner eat a flipping face flannel than a **lettuce**.

"No?" said Grandpa.

"Not really, no," said Norm.

"What about carrots, then?"

Yeah, thought Norm. What **about** flipping carrots?

"Tomatoes?" said Grandpa.

Norm shook his head. As far as he was concerned, the only place a tomato belonged was sliced and on top of a pizza. Apart from that? Forget it.

"Hmmm," said Grandpa, stroking his chin thoughtfully, like a movie villain hatching some kind of cunning plan. "Just how annoying **were** they, would you say? On a scale of one to ten?"

"You mean my cousins?" said Norm uncertainly.

"No, I mean the **carrots**," said Grandpa.

"Uh?" said Norm.

"Of **course** I mean your cousins, you numpty."

"Oh, right," said Norm. "Eleven."

"Eleven, eh?" said Grandpa.

At **least**, thought Norm, as Grandpa did a bit more chin-stroking. Frankly there wasn't a scale

big enough to accurately convey **just** how annoying his cousins were. And anyway, what had any of this got to do with **food**? That's what **Norm** wanted to know.

"Get your butt round here, Norman."

"Pardon?" said Norm.

"You heard," said Grandpa. "Get your butt round here. I need you to do something for me."

"But..."

"No buts," said Grandpa. "I said get your butt round here. Now."

"'Kay," said Norm doing as he was told and pedalling off towards the main entrance.

"Kids today," said Grandpa, disappearing into his shed and emerging a few seconds later carrying an empty bucket.

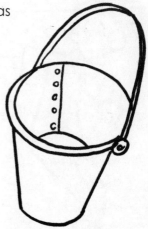

"What's that for?" said Norm, cycling up the path.

"For carrying things in," said Grandpa. "Don't they teach you **anything** at school these days?"

"What?" said Norm, braking and stopping. "No, I know what a **bucket's** for, Grandpa. But what's it got to do with **me**?"

Grandpa looked at Norm for a moment. "How do you know the bucket's got **anything** to do with you?"

"**Has** it?" said Norm.

Grandpa nodded. "It has actually. I want you to fill it."

"Uh?" said Norm. "From **here**? But..."

"What?" said Grandpa.

"I don't **need** the toilet, Grandpa."

"**What?**" said Grandpa, pulling a face. "No, I don't want you to **pee** in it!"

"Oh, right," said Norm. "So..."

"I want you to fill it with **snails**."

Norm waited a couple of seconds whilst his brain processed this information. Or at least, whilst his brain **tried** to process this information. Had Grandpa just said what he **thought** he'd just said, or had he imagined it? In fact, come to think of it, thought Norm, coming to think of it, had he imagined the whole flipping day so far? Because it was beginning to seem like he might have done.

"Erm, did you just say **snails**, Grandpa?"

"Correct," said Grandpa.

"You want me to fill that bucket, with **snails**?"

"That's right."

"Actual **snails**?" said Norm.

"Actual **snails**," said Grandpa. "Molluscs."

Norm looked at Grandpa. "**Molluscs**?"

Grandpa nodded. "A group of invertebrates that also includes slugs, clams and oysters, as well as squid, octopuses and cuttlefish. Molluscs."

Never mind the **molluscs**, thought Norm. Because for **one** thing, if he'd wanted a precise dictionary definition, he'd have flipping **Googled** it. And secondly, what Grandpa was suggesting, was, without shadow of a doubt, one of the grossest things he'd ever heard in his life. And that **included** the time he'd walked past the front room and heard his mum and dad snogging each other. At least he'd **assumed** it was snogging that he'd heard. Either that or there'd been a problem with the plumbing.

"Where am I going to find a bunch of snails?"

"Funny you should ask," said Grandpa.

It wasn't **funny**, thought Norm. It was unbe-flipping-**lievable!**

"And it's not a **bunch** of snails, either," said Grandpa. "It's a **rout** of snails. Or an **escargatoire** of snails."

"What?" said Norm.

"The collective noun for snails," said Grandpa. "It's not a **bunch**. It's a **rout**, or **escargatoire**."

Gordon flipping **Bennet**, thought Norm. Who **cared** what the flipping collective whatsit was, for snails? And anyway, how did Grandpa even **know** that? Where did you **learn** that kind of stuff? More importantly, why would you even **want** to learn that kind of stuff? It wasn't the kind of thing you were ever likely to drop into everyday conversation, was it? Well, not as far as Norm was concerned it wasn't, anyway.

"And by the way, you'll find them everywhere."

"***Everywhere?***" said Norm.

"Here, in the allotments," said Grandpa, nodding. "And they're a right nuisance, let me tell you. Munching on my veg."

A ***nuisance***? thought Norm. Never mind ***nuisance***. Anything that spent their days munching away on ***vegetables*** had to be out of their flipping ***minds***.

If snails actually **had** minds, in the first place. And they probably didn't. Grandpa would no doubt know if they did, or not. But there was no flipping **way** Norm was going to ask him. Not now, anyway. Or ever, actually. There was only so much snail-related knowledge a guy could take. And Norm was already at his limit.

"Why, Grandpa?"

"Why?" said Grandpa.

"Yeah," said Norm. "Why do you want me to fill a bucket with snails?"

"Well, that's a reasonable question, I suppose, Norman."

Yes, thought Norm. It **was** a reasonable question. Not only that, but it was a question he never thought he'd have to ask.

"You scratch my back and I'll scratch yours," said Grandpa.

Uh? thought Norm. What on earth was Grandpa

 on about **now**? His back didn't even **need** scratching! This was all beginning to do his flipping **head** in!

"You look confused," said Grandpa.

"Do I?" said Norm.

"It's very simple," said Grandpa. "You get your hands dirty – or slimy, anyway – and I'll go and get you something to eat."

"Oh, right. I **see**."

"Deal, or no deal?"

"Erm…deal, I suppose," said Norm, mainly because he couldn't think of a good enough excuse **not** to. Well, he probably **could** have done. But not until later. And later would be too late. He needed an excuse **now**.

"Excellent," said Grandpa, handing Norm the bucket. "Better get cracking then, hadn't you?"

"Can I ask you a question, Grandpa?" said Norm.

"I don't know," said Grandpa, his eyes crinkling slightly in the corners. "*Can* you?"

"Why don't you just spray them with some...some...stuff?"

"The snails?" said Grandpa.

"No," said Norm. "The *carrots*."

"Very funny," said Grandpa. "Have you ever thought of being a comedian?"

"Nah," said Norm.

"Just as well."

"What?" said Norm.

"I don't actually want to **kill** the snails."

Norm thought for a moment. "Wait, Grandpa. Have you gone..."

"Nuts?" said Grandpa.

"No," said Norm. "Vegetarian."

"Same thing," said Grandpa.

"So, **have** you?"

"Me? Vegetarian?" said Grandpa as if Norm had just asked whether he liked hip-hop. "No way, José!"

"So what's wrong with killing snails, then?"

"Seriously, Norman?"

"Seriously," said Norm.

"Just because I eat meat doesn't mean I go round **killing** things willy-nilly."

Norm couldn't help giggling.

"What's so funny?" said Grandpa.

"Nothing," said Norm.

"Oh, wait," said Grandpa. "Is it because I said **willy**-nilly?"

Norm giggled again.

"How old are you, Norman?"

"Nearly thirteen," said Norm.

Grandpa thought for a moment. "That explains it."

"So why **don't** you...you know...spray them?" said Norm.

"Because I want to **recycle** them, that's why."

Norm was confused. "**Recycle** them?"

Grandpa nodded.

"But..."

"What?"

"How can you **recycle** snails, Grandpa?"

"Ah," said Grandpa, disappearing down the path. "That's for me to know and you to find out, isn't it, Norman?"

Is it? thought Norm. Did he **really** want to know how snails could be recycled? Because if so, his life had just hit an all-time flipping low.

CHAPTER 9

As Norm cycled home, he reflected on the day so far. Or at least, he reflected on **his** day so far. He had no idea what everyone **else** had been up to. And frankly, he had very little **interest** in what everyone else had been up to. And even if he **had**, how would he have found out, without actually **asking** them all? Facebook?

It had certainly been an **interesting** day so far, thought Norm as he turned the corner and began pedalling down the street towards his house. Well, interesting **and** annoying, thanks mainly to his flipping cousins suddenly appearing. But from the moment he'd woken up – and found himself home alone – to hanging his mum's frilly pants out to dry and then picking snails off cabbage leaves, it had been...well, it had been a **different** kind of day. Not that that was necessarily a **bad** thing, thought Norm. And not that he'd actually **known** he was

picking snails off **cabbage** leaves, of course. As far as **Norm** was concerned, he was merely picking snails off green things that grew out of the ground. Frankly, they could have been just about **anything**. It wasn't as if he had the slightest intention of ever actually **eating** them. Especially after they'd been slimed on and crawled over by a load of molluscs, or whatever it was that Grandpa called them.

The bucket had been nowhere near full of snails by the time Grandpa returned to the allotment. But Grandpa didn't seem to mind. He'd said that there were 'enough'. Enough for what exactly, he *didn't* say. But it was all Norm needed to know. He could stop. He'd stuck to *his* side of the deal. Even *better*, Grandpa had stuck to *his* side of the deal and bought not only a truly *massive* bottle of cola, but an enormous packet of Jammie Dodgers, as well. And not only *that*, but it wasn't even supermarket own-brand cola – and they *weren't* even supermarket own-brand Jammie Dodgers, either. It was *proper* cola – and they were *proper*, one hundred per cent *genuine* Jammie Dodgers, manufactured, as far as Norm could tell, in the *actual* Jammie Dodger

factory! Life – or at least **Norm's** life, anyway – was suddenly looking up. If only temporarily.

"Hello, **Norman**!" shrieked Chelsea, suddenly popping up on the other side of the fence, the second Norm wheelied up the drive.

"GORDON FLIPPING **BENNET**!" yelled Norm, wobbling and very nearly smashing into the garage door.

Chelsea grinned. "Did you miss me?"

"No," said Norm, quickly.

"Charming," said Chelsea. "You might have at least **thought** about it."

"I flipping **did** think about it," said Norm.

"Now, now, **Norman**," said Chelsea. "There's no need for that."

But there flipping well **was**, thought Norm. Trust **her** to bring him crashing straight back down to earth again. Almost **literally** crashing straight back down to earth, as it happened. But then, what was flipping **new**? Something rubbish **always** followed something good. Well, at least in **Norm's** experience it did, anyway. Almost like it was some kind of flipping **law**, or something. Why, just for once, couldn't something even **better** follow something good? And something even **better** after **that**? That was what **Norm** wanted to know. And it wasn't like having proper cola and Jammie Dodgers was the most **incredible** experience ever. To **most** people that was probably a perfectly average everyday kind of an experience. But to **Norm** it was the equivalent of **all** his Christmases and birthdays coming at once **and** winning the flipping lottery.

So surely it wasn't **too** much to expect something else at least **half**-decent to happen before the next rubbish thing, was it?

"What was that you were trying to do, anyway?" said Chelsea.

"What do you mean, **trying** to do?" said Norm, immediately feeling his blood beginning to boil.

"When you came up the drive?"

"You mean, doing a wheelie?"

Chelsea giggled. "Doing a wee-wee?"

Norm sighed. "Not a **wee-wee**. A **wheelie**!"

"What's the point of that, then?"

Norm pulled a face. "What's the point of a **wheelie**?"

Chelsea grinned. "Well I already know what the point of a **wee-wee** is!"

"I don't understand what you mean," said Norm.

"Well, I mean, you've got two wheels, haven't you?"

"Yeah? So?" said Norm.

"So why not **use** them both, then?" said Chelsea.

"What?" said Norm.

"Relax, **Norman**! I'm just pulling your **leg**."

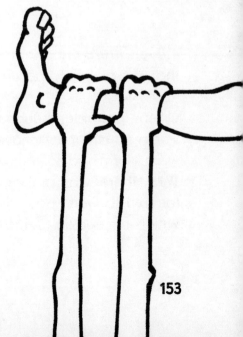

153

In the back of Norm's mind, he knew that Chelsea really **was** pulling his leg. Not only that, but he knew that Chelsea knew that he knew that she really was pulling his leg. But that **still** didn't stop her from winding him up and making him want to headbutt the nearest bus. Which somehow made

it even **more** annoying. But then, thought Norm, that was probably the whole idea.

On the plus side, though, Chelsea was still only a flipping **fraction** as annoying as his perfect cousins were. Norm had no idea what that precise fraction **was**. There was probably some kind of stupid formula to work it out, if he could be bothered. Which he couldn't. **And** if he was any good at maths. Which he **wasn't**. All Norm knew was that no **one** individual on the planet could **ever** be as annoying as his three perfect cousins combined.

"Where have you been, anyway?" said Chelsea.

"Uh?" grunted Norm like a startled gibbon.

"Where have you been?"

"None of your flipping business," said Norm.

"All right, all right, Captain Grumpyknickers!" said Chelsea. "Who's rattled **your** cage, all of a sudden?"

All of a **sudden**? thought Norm. She'd been rattling his flipping cage for as long as he could remember, along with just about everybody **else** he knew! It was a minor miracle there were any bars left on his cage to actually **be** rattled!

"Seriously," said Chelsea. "You look as if someone just puked on your pizza!"

Gordon flipping **Bennet**, thought Norm, doing his best to delete that particular image from his mind. Hardly surprising, either, given Norm's lifelong passion for pretty much **any** kind of pizza. But if he ever saw **that** flavour on the menu, even **he'd** give it a miss.

"Well?" said Chelsea, who wasn't used to taking 'no' for an answer – and who didn't look like she was going to on this occasion, either.

Norm sighed, wearily. "You got any cousins?"

Chelsea shrugged. "Yeah, I have actually. But I hardly ever see them."

"You're flipping *lucky*, then," said Norm.

"Ah," said Chelsea. "So *that's* what it is then."

Norm sighed again, if anything, even *more* wearily than the time before.

"They've gone, by the way."

"What?" said Norm.

"They've gone," said Chelsea.

"Who have?"

"Your cousins."

"Really?" said Norm.

"Yeah. They left a while ago."

Norm looked at Chelsea for a moment, desperately *wanting* to believe that what she'd just said was true, but still not quite convinced that it actually *was* true. Knowing Chelsea, this could *easily* be some kind of wind-up. In fact, thought Norm,

157

knowing Chelsea, it probably **was** some kind of wind-up.

"How do you know?"

"I know **everything**," said Chelsea mysteriously.

"Uh? What?" said Norm.

"I **saw** them, silly-billy!"

Silly-billy? thought Norm. How old did she think he was? Flipping **two**, or something? But he couldn't let anything **else** annoy him. Not now, anyway. What he needed **now** was actual **proof** that his cousins had gone. Because if they **had**, that would be the best news since...since...well, since Grandpa had bought the cola and the Jammie Dodgers, about half an hour ago.

"How do you know they were my cousins?"

"Well, I don't know for **sure**," said Chelsea.

"How many of them were there?" said Norm.

"Three," said Chelsea. "Plus two adults."

"Was one of the adults a bit…?"

"A bit **what**?" said Chelsea. "Hoity-toity?"

"What?" said Norm.

"Stuck-up looking?" said Chelsea.

Norm nodded.

"The mum, you mean?"

Norm nodded again, much more vigorously.

"**Definitely**!" said Chelsea. "She was acting like she was the **Queen**, or something."

Bingo! thought Norm.

"And they all got into this really **cool**-looking car."

159

Norm turned around. He hadn't noticed before, but the car was gone.

"Well?" said Chelsea.

"Yep, that was them," said Norm.

"See?" said Chelsea. "Told you."

"They're so flipping annoying," said Norm.

"Why?" said Chelsea.

"**Why?**" said Norm as if this was the most ridiculous question he'd ever been asked. "How long have you **got**?"

"Let me see, now," said Chelsea, looking at her watch. "Couple of hours? Maybe more."

Norm was horrified. A couple of **hours**? Firstly, he'd sooner eat freshly puked-on **pizza** than spend a couple more **minutes** with **Chelsea**, let alone a couple more **hours**. And

secondly, that was nowhere **near** long enough to even **begin** telling her just what it was that he found so unbe-flipping-**lievably** annoying about his perfect flipping cousins. It would be much quicker to tell her what he didn't find annoying about them. Because there was practically nothing Norm **didn't** find deeply and intensely annoying and mind-bogglingly **irritating** about his perfect flipping cousins.

"Well?" said Chelsea expectantly.

"Everything," said Norm.

Chelsea grinned. "**Everything?**"

Norm nodded. "Everything."

"Can you be a bit more…specific?" said Chelsea.

"Uh?" said Norm.

"Can you give me an **example** of why you find them annoying?"

"Not really, no," said Norm.

"Fair enough," said Chelsea.

Norm thought for a moment.

"Actually, there is one thing."

"Ooh goody, I'm all ears," said Chelsea.

"They've gone vegetarian," said Norm.

"Riiiiiight," said Chelsea. "And?"

Norm pulled a face. "What do you mean, **and**? And **nothing**. That's it."

Chelsea tilted her head and studied Norm for a few seconds. "That's **it**?"

"Yeah," said Norm.

"Erm…"

"What?" said Norm.

"What's so annoying about going vegetarian?"

Norm looked at Chelsea as if she'd just asked what was so annoying about **homework**. "Seriously?"

"Seriously," said Chelsea. "Because in case you didn't know, **Norman**, I'm vegetarian, too."

No, thought Norm. He **didn't** know that. Why **would** he have known that? He'd never had to flipping **eat** with Chelsea before, thank flipping goodness. It was bad enough having to live next **door** to her!

"Are you saying that **I'm** annoying, as well?" said Chelsea.

All of a sudden Norm felt like a rabbit caught in the beam of a car's headlights. Not that Norm actually knew what that felt like, of course. Who did, apart from an actual rabbit caught in the beam of a car's headlights? And presumably not too many of **those** lived to tell the tale afterwards. And not that rabbits could talk, anyway. But that wasn't the point. The point was that Norm was suddenly frozen with indecision. What should he say? Yes, he found Chelsea annoying? Which he *did*. Or no, he *didn't* find her annoying? Which would be lying?

"If you have to *think* about it, then you've just answered my question," said Chelsea.

"Have I?" said Norm uncertainly.

"Yes," said Chelsea. "You obviously think that I *am* annoying!"

"Erm..."

Chelsea grinned.

"What's so funny?" said Norm.

"You look cute when you're worried, **Norman**."

Gordon flipping **Bennet**, thought Norm. In that case he must make sure that he never ever looked worried again, for the rest of his flipping life. Even if deep down inside he was abso-flipping-lutely **petrified**. At least, not when Chelsea was around, anyway. Which hopefully wouldn't be **all** that often, in the future. But even so, this was an extremely worrying development. No, no! thought Norm, immediately correcting himself. Not a **worrying** development! But certainly an **unexpected** development.

"Anyway, I don't care if you think I'm annoying," said Chelsea.

"Really?" said Norm. "Well, that's all right, then."

"Oh, so you really **do** think I'm annoying, then?"

"Erm, well—" began Norm.

"It's OK," said Chelsea, cutting him off. "I'm just pulling your leg again."

Norm sighed. At this rate, Chelsea was going to end up pulling his flipping leg right **off**.

"I'm not **really** vegetarian."

"Uh? What?" said Norm.

Chelsea shrugged. "I'm not really vegetarian."

"Oh, right," said Norm.

"But I could be, if I wanted to."

And what was **that** supposed to mean? thought Norm. **He** could be flipping vegetarian, if he **wanted** to! He could do all **sorts** of things, if he **wanted** to! He could march up and down the street totally naked and playing the flipping

bagpipes if he **wanted** to! But luckily, he **didn't** want to. Well, luckily for the neighbours, he didn't want to, anyway. But that wasn't the point.

"Anyway, I **still** don't see what's so annoying about it," said Chelsea. "Each to their own and all that. Live and let live. If you'll pardon the pun."

Uh? thought Norm. What flipping pun was that, then? He had no idea what she was **talking** about any more. Not that he **ever** had all that much idea what Chelsea was talking about. But now it was almost as if she was going out of her way to confuse him. And so far, she was doing a pretty decent job of it, too.

"Oh, **there** you are," said Norm's mum, poking her head out of the front door. "I've been looking **everywhere** for you!"

Everywhere? thought Norm. She obviously hadn't looked in the **allotments**.

"Hi!" trilled Chelsea.

"Oh hello, Chelsea!" said Norm's mum. "Didn't see you there. How are you?"

"Fine, thanks!" said Chelsea.

Norm's mum turned back to Norm and scrutinised him for a moment.

"What?" said Norm.

"You **have** been in your room, haven't you?"

"Yeah, **course** I have, Mum," said Norm. Which, technically speaking, was true. He **had** been in his room. Loads of times. Just not recently.

"It's just that you look a little…"

"What, Mum?"

"Out of breath?"

"Really?" said Norm. "Do I?"

Norm's mum nodded. "And guilty."

"Guilty?" said Norm.

"You're not trying to pull the wool over my eyes, are you?"

"What?"

"You're not telling porkies?"

"No, really, Mum," said Norm. "I've only just got here. Haven't I, Chelsea?"

"Pardon?" said Chelsea.

"I said I've only just got here, **haven't** I?" said Norm, winking at Chelsea, but making sure that his mum couldn't see. Because all of a sudden Norm needed Chelsea's help. Otherwise he could be in serious trouble here. And right now, Norm needed more trouble like he needed a flipping hole in the head. It had seemed perfectly reasonable at the time, leaving the house instead of going to his room as his mum had probably intended. It hadn't seemed like that big a deal. But now, all of a sudden, Norm wasn't quite so sure. The question was, did Chelsea *know* that? Was she on the same wavelength as him? Would she play along with it? After all, there was no particular *reason* why she *should*. He'd just made it pretty clear that he thought she was dead annoying. OK, so she *said* she didn't care. But *did* she care, deep down? Norm had a funny feeling he was about to find out.

"Well, Chelsea?" said Norm's mum. "Has he?"

Chelsea smiled sweetly and nodded. "Yes, he has."

Norm looked at Chelsea with a mixture of relief and gratitude. Which was unusual for a start, because he was far more used to looking at her with a mixture of barely controlled rage and simmering resentment. But, at that precise moment, Norm could have happily *kissed* Chelsea. Well, maybe not **happily** kissed her. But kissed her without actually being **paid** to do it, anyway.

"Sorry, love," said Norm's mum.

"I'm quite hurt, actually," said Norm.

"Really?"

"Yeah, really," said Norm. And it was true. He **was** hurt. Why had his mum believed **Chelsea**, but not **him**? OK, so it was a complete load of **nonsense**. He **hadn't** actually been in his room all this time, at all. He'd been out on his bike. But that was beside the point. He was his mum's **son**! Her own flesh and flipping **blood**. Flipping **typical**.

"I'd like a word, by the way."

Norm shrugged, but showed no sign of moving. "'Kay."

"I mean, I'd like a word, *inside*," said his mum.

"Oh, right," said Norm.

"Bye, Chelsea!" called Norm's mum, disappearing back into the house.

"Bye!" trilled Chelsea before turning to Norm.

"What?" said Norm.

"Well, that's a shame, isn't it?"

"What is?"

Chelsea smiled. "Well, I mean, you've only just come out and now you've got to go straight back in?"

"Oh right, yeah," said Norm.

"Don't worry, **Norman**," said Chelsea with a wink. "Your secret's safe with me."

"Really?" said Norm uncertainly, as if he didn't quite believe her.

"Yeah, course," said Chelsea.

Norm sighed with relief. "Thanks."

"I should think so, too, **Norman**!"

"I owe you one."

"You certainly **do**."

"Hurry up, love!" called Norm's mum.

"Coming, Mum," said Norm, leaning his bike against the wall before heading towards the door.

CHAPTER 10

"We're in here!" called Norm's dad, as Norm walked through the front door and automatically began heading for the kitchen.

Norm stopped and sighed. Not only had he not realised that **both** his parents had wanted a word with him, but the fact that they wanted a word with him, in the **front room**, immediately spelled danger. Well, strictly speaking, D.A.N.G.E.R. spelled **danger** but the point was, if he ever got summoned to the front room by his parents, it was usually bad news. Or at least, bad news as far as **Norm** was concerned.

"I said we're—"

"Coming," said Norm, saving his dad the bother of finishing the sentence.

"What kept you?" said Norm's mum, when Norm finally appeared.

Norm shrugged. "Dunno. I just…"

"Sit down," said Norm's dad. "We've got something to tell you."

This really didn't look good at all, thought Norm, doing as he was told and sitting down in the nearest available chair. Not the chair. The chair looked perfectly fine. It was just a chair, after all. But what on earth were his parents about to tell him? That

they were selling the house and moving to an even **smaller** one? That **he'd** been put up for sale? That...that...that... No, wait, thought Norm. Surely not. His mum wasn't having another **baby**, was she? Not at **her** age? Because that would be just about the grossest thing imaginable.

"Don't worry, love," said Norm's mum. "It's not **that** bad!"

"Uh? What?" said Norm. "So you're not ..."

"Not what?"

"Having a ..."

"Having a **what?**" said Norm's mum.

"Nothing," said Norm, breathing a huge mental sigh of relief.

"We've been thinking," said Norm's dad.

"Really?" said Norm. "What about, Dad?"

"About what Auntie Jem was saying."

Norm looked at his dad for a moment. Was that the very slightest glimmer of a smile he detected? If it was, then it was over and done with in the blink of an eye. Well, depending on how quickly eyes actually blinked, of course. But the point was, if it **was** a glimmer of a smile, it was an extremely **quick** one.

"Shall I tell him, or do you want to do it?"

"I'll do it," said his mum.

"Sure?" said Norm's dad.

Norm's mum nodded. "Sure."

Gordon flipping **Bennet**! thought Norm, who personally couldn't give two flipping hoots **who** told him. As long as one of them did. And soon. Because the suspense was beginning to do his noggin in.

"We're going vegetarian, love," said his mum.

"WHAAAAAAAT?" roared Norm as if he'd just been told that from now on, not only was he going to have to go to the toilet *publicly*, it was going to be televised live.

"You heard, love," said Norm's mum calmly. "We're going vegetarian."

There was a brief moment of silence before Norm suddenly burst out laughing like a hysterical hyena.

"Yeah, good one, Mum!" he just about managed to splutter, between hastily gulped breaths.

"What do you mean, *good one*?" said Norm's mum. "We're serious."

Norm looked at his mum. Then at his dad. Then at his mum again.

"You're not *serious*, are you?"

Norm's mum was confused. "Pardon?"

"Are you *serious* that you're serious?" said Norm.

"Am I *serious* that I'm serious?"

Norm nodded. "Yeah."

"Of *course* I'm serious," said Norm's mum.

Norm *still* wasn't *completely* convinced that he wasn't the subject of some kind of elaborate prank or hoax, and that he wasn't being secretly filmed for some stupid TV show, or that this whole thing wasn't somehow going to end up on flipping YouTube.

"*Seriously?*"

Norm's mum looked even **more** confused. "Pardon?"

"You're not joking?" said Norm.

"No, love. I'm not joking."

Norm sighed like he'd never sighed before.

"I wouldn't joke about something as important as **this**, would I?"

No, thought Norm. She flipping well **wouldn't** joke about something as important as this. Firstly, it would be a pretty rubbish joke. And secondly? *AA AAAAAAAAAAAAAAAAAAA AAAAAAAAAAAAAAAAA AAA AAAAAAAAAAAAAAAAAAAAAAAA AAAAAAAAAAAAAAAAAAAAAAAAGH!*

"What's the matter?" said Norm's dad.

What was the matter? thought Norm. What was the flipping **matter**? **Everything** was the flipping matter. **Everything**. And no. He **couldn't** be more flipping pacific. Or whatever that stupid fancy word was that Chelsea had said a few minutes ago.

"Well?" said Norm's dad.

Norm opened his mouth to say something, but nothing came out. Then again it wasn't **easy** speaking when you'd just heard that your world was about to end and that life as you knew it would never **ever** be the same again.

"What do you think?" said his dad.

"WHY?" wailed Norm like an overtired toddler on the verge of a massive tantrum.

"Because I want to know what you **think**, Norman. **That's** why."

"Uh?" said Norm. "No, I mean **why** are we going flipping **vegetarian**, Dad?"

"Oh, I see," began Norm's dad. "Well, firstly there's no need for language. And secondly…"

Norm's dad stopped, mid-sentence, and frowned, as if whatever he was about to say wasn't going to be very **easy** to say. And possibly not easy for anyone else to **hear**, either.

"The thing is…" he said, before stopping again.

What? thought Norm. **What** was the flipping thing? Because as far as **he** could see, the thing was that his mum and dad had just gone stark, raving, round the twist, full-on flipping **bonkers** with flipping

knobs on. What other possible explanation could there be?

"The thing ***is***, love…" said Norm's mum, carrying on where his dad had left off. "Auntie Jem was…"

"Bang out of order?" said Norm's dad.

"Well, I don't know if I'd go quite ***that*** far," said his mum.

"Oh, really?" said Norm's dad. "Well, ***I*** would. It was humiliating, being told how to live our lives."

"I'm not sure she actually ***meant*** to humiliate us," said Norm's mum.

Maybe not, thought Norm. But amazingly, he actually agreed with his dad for once. It ***was*** pretty humiliating. And it ***was*** bang out of order.

"And at the end of the day…" began Norm's mum.

What? thought Norm. It got dark? Everyone went to bed?

"She was right."

Norm looked at his mum, almost willing her to finally burst out laughing and admit that it really *was* all a joke. But she didn't.

"Auntie Jem was *right*. Being vegetarian *is* healthier for you. And it actually *could*..."

"Be the worst decision you ever make?" said Norm.

"No, love."

Norm shrugged. "*What* then, Mum?"

"Well, it *could* actually save us *money*. Money which could be spent on *other* things."

Norm considered this for a moment. Or rather, he considered some of the 'other things' the money could possibly be spent on, for a moment. Like his bike, for instance. Because if he ever really *was* to become World Mountain Biking Champion, his *current* bike was going to need some *serious* pimping up. And *soon*. Because for a start it needed some new front forks. *And* some new brakes. And it would be a bit of a waste to put **new** brakes on **old** wheels, wouldn't it? So why not just get a nice new pair of super-light alloy rims, whilst he was at it? And a new super-**duper** lightweight carbon frame, too? In fact, come to think of it, why not just get a brand spanking new flipping **bike**, whilst he was at it? Preferably one of the ones he'd been drooling over on his iPad. It would be **so** much easier. **But**, thought Norm, it would also be a **heck** of a price to pay. Not the actual price of the bike bit. Although that **would** actually be a heck of a price, too. The actual going **vegetarian** bit. That would be even **more** of a **heck** of a price to pay! Could he actually **do** it, at the end of the day? Or at **any** time of the day, for that matter? Because if all he was going to eat from now on was flipping **rabbit** food, there'd be no **point** getting a new bike, because he probably wouldn't have the strength to get **on** it, let alone actually **ride** it!

"It's true," said Norm's dad.

"Uh? What is?" said Norm distractedly.

"What your mum just said. It **could** save us money. And, well… You don't need **me** to tell you that money's been a bit hard to come by, lately, Norman."

No, **really**? thought Norm sarcastically. Could have flipping fooled **him**. He'd just assumed they'd moved to this stupid micro sized house and started eating own-brand flipping **Coco** Pops, for the sheer **fun** of it. It had never even **occurred** to him that it **might** have had something to do with the fact that they were completely skint and didn't have two flipping **beans** to rub together. Though why anyone would actually **want** to rub two flipping **beans** together in the first place was a mystery to **Norm**. And anyway, thought Norm, whose flipping fault **was** it that money had been 'a bit hard to come by' lately? His flipping **dad's**! And by the way, never mind **hard** to come by. Money had been almost **impossible** to come by, lately.

"She still shouldn't have said it, though."

"Uh? What?" said Norm. "Who shouldn't? You mean..."

"Auntie Jem," said Norm's dad, nodding.

"Certainly not in front of you and your brothers, she shouldn't, anyway," added Norm's mum.

"Like I said," said his dad. "It was bang out of order."

"Well, yes, **perhaps**," said Norm's mum. "But even so, **you** shouldn't have said what **you** said either, Norman."

Norm looked genuinely mystified. "What do you mean, Mum?"

"Don't tell me you can't remember?"

OK, thought Norm. He wouldn't.

"Telling Danny to shut up?" said Norm's mum.

"Oh, that," said Norm. "But—"

"Uh-uh, no buts," said his mum, cutting him off with a wag of a finger. "I've literally **never** been so embarrassed."

Whoa, thought Norm. His mum thought **that** was embarrassing?

She should try being **him** for a day. **Then** she'd know what flipping **embarrassing** was!

"Really, Mum?"

"Really what?"

"You've **literally** never been so embarrassed?"

Norm's mum nodded. "I've **literally** never been so embarrassed."

"But—"

"Uh-uh!" said Norm's mum with another wag of her finger. "I said 'no buts', Norman! And if I say it was **embarrassing**? It was **embarrassing**. End of."

"Yeah, whatever," muttered Norm.

"**Excuse** me?" said Norm's mum, beginning to look and sound quite cross.

"Nothing," said Norm.

"Are you just going to let him talk to me like that, or are you actually going to **do** something?" said Norm's mum, shooting his dad a disapproving look.

It was a good question actually, thought Norm. **Was** his dad just going to let him talk to his mum like that? Because normally he'd have been down on him like a ton of flipping **bricks**, by now and telling him to apologise and not to be so cheeky and all that stuff. So why **hadn't** he? wondered Norm. Not that he was **complaining**, of course. Far from it. It just seemed a little...out of character for his dad, that was all.

"Well," said Norm's mum. "**Are** you?"

"Erm...don't

talk to your mother like that, son," said Norm's dad, rather half-heartedly.

"And..." said Norm's mum.

"Say sorry," said his dad.

"Sorry?" said Norm.

"I **said**, say sorry."

Norm sighed. "Sorry, Mum."

"I should think so, too," said Norm's mum. "I doubt they'll be back any time—"

"Pardon?" said Norm, not quite daring to believe what he'd just heard. Or rather, **believing** what he'd just heard, but not quite daring to believe that what he'd just heard actually **meant** what he **hoped** it meant. "You mean..."

"Yes," said Norm's mum. "Your cousins. And Auntie Jem and Uncle Steve, of course. I doubt they'll be back any time—"

"**Seriously?**" said Norm, doing his best not to get **too** excited. At least on the **outside**, anyway. On the **inside** it was a different matter altogether. On the **inside** he was having a flipping **party!**

"Let me **finish**!" said Norm's mum. "You keep on interrupting me!"

"Sorry, Mum," said Norm.

"As I was saying," said Norm's mum. "Or as I was **trying** to say, anyway. I doubt they'll be back any time **soon**."

"Oh, I see," said Norm, instantly deflated again as if he'd suddenly got a puncture. Well, as if his **bike** had suddenly got a puncture, anyway. Not **him**.

Norm's mum looked puzzled.

"I mean...oh, that's **good**, then," said Norm. "Because that would be a real shame if they **never** visited us again, Mum. Obviously."

"Well, yes, obviously," said his mum. "They're family, after all."

Allegedly, thought Norm.

"But we've digressed," said Norm's mum.

Norm pulled a face. He had no idea whether they'd digressed, or not. Mainly because he had no flipping idea what **digressed** actually **meant**. Unless it had something to do with **digestive**? But that was a kind of biscuit, wasn't it?

"We've **deviated** from the original subject," said his mum, sensing Norm's confusion.

"Oh, right," said Norm.

"We were **supposed** to be talking about going **vegetarian**, not about your **cousins**," said Norm's mum, as if he could have somehow already **forgotten**. Which, on the one hand, was quite possible. In fact, not just **possible**. Quite **likely**. Because Norm **was** notoriously forgetful. As Grandpa had said on more than one occasion, he'd forget his head if it wasn't screwed on properly. **Norm**, that is. Not **Grandpa**. And not that Norm's head really **was** screwed on, of course. It was just another one of Grandpa's funny expressions. But on the **other** hand, even **Norm** was unlikely to have already forgotten the monu-flipping-**mental** bombshell his mum had just casually lobbed into the conversation, as if it really wasn't that big a deal at all. But it really **was** a big deal. It was a

humongous, visible from flipping **space**-sized deal. At least to **Norm** it was, anyway.

"Don't worry," said Norm's dad. "We're not going to do it just like that."

"Just like **what**?" said Norm.

"Just like **that**," said Norm's dad, with a click of his fingers. "We don't think it would be very sensible to **suddenly** go vegetarian."

At least they were agreed on **something** then, thought Norm. Well, **almost** agreed on something, anyway. **He** didn't think it would be sensible to go vegetarian at **all**, never mind flipping **suddenly**.

"Your dad's right," said Norm's mum. "It wouldn't be very fair on your brothers."

"What?" said Norm.

"Brian and Dave?" said his mum.

Gordon flipping **Bennet**, thought Norm. He knew who his flipping **brothers** were! He wasn't **that** flipping forgetful! Not **quite** anyway.

"It wouldn't be fair on them if we did it too quickly."

Flipping **typical**, thought Norm. Never mind **him**! Never mind how **he** felt! It was **all** about his stupid little **brothers**. Same as flipping **usual**!

196

"So we think it's probably best if we introduce it slowly."

Slowly? thought Norm. They could introduce it one sprout at a flipping time over the next fifty flipping **years** for all **he** cared. It didn't make what they were doing any less cruel and inhumane. It didn't make it any less like some kind of weird medieval torture. In fact, if anything, it made it even **more** like some kind of weird medieval torture. The actual **speed** they were introducing it made no difference whatso-flipping-**ever!** They were still flipping introducing it, weren't they? And if his parents had the slightest shred of humanity in them – which they clearly **didn't** – they had to stop this madness

Sprout-O-Matic

197

now. If only there was a way to make them change their sick, twisted minds.

Actually, thought Norm. Perhaps there ***was*** a way.

"What if I'm allergic to it?"

"Allergic to what?" said Norm's mum.

Norm shrugged. "Vegetarians."

Norm's mum pulled a face. "Do you mean vegetarians or ***vegetarianism***?"

Norm thought for a moment. He'd ***meant*** what if he was allergic to vegetarianism? Or at least, he ***thought*** that's what he'd meant. But thinking about it, what if he was allergic to actual vegetarians, too? Maybe ***that*** was why he'd reacted so badly when his perfect cousins had been around earlier! Maybe if he ***hadn't*** been told to leave the room he'd have come out in a flipping rash! It did seem a ***little*** unlikely. But frankly, thought Norm, who flipping ***cared***? He certainly didn't. Not if it meant there was even the faintest sliver of a chance that his parents would change their minds.

"Well?" said Norm's mum.

"Both," said Norm. "Either. Whatever."

"It's doubtful you'd be allergic to **all** vegetarian food, love," said his mum.

"Wanna bet?" mumbled Norm.

"Well, we're going to give it a try," said Norm's dad. "See how we get on."

Norm could feel what little resistance he still had fading away, like the last rays of daylight as the

sun finally dipped below the horizon. His shoulders slumped even more than usual. It seemed like there really was **nothing** he could do.

"What's the worst that could happen?" said Norm's dad.

What was the worst that could **happen**? thought Norm. Apart from turning green and his heading spinning round and projectile vomiting carrots and flipping sweetcorn everywhere?

"I've been looking at some recipes actually," said Norm's mum.

"Really?" said Norm, with a growing sense of dread.

"Yes, really. I think you're going to be pleasantly surprised, love."

Norm sighed. The only way **he** was going to be pleasantly surprised was if he actually **survived**.

"Come on," said Norm's dad, getting up and heading towards the door. "Into the car."

"Uh?" said Norm. "The car? Why, Dad? Where are we going?"

"To the supermarket. We need to get a few bits and bobs for dinner."

"But..." began Norm.

"What?" said his dad.

"Why do I need to come?"

"Because you **do**," said Norm's dad. "And that's all there is to it."

Gordon flipping **Bennet**, thought Norm, getting up and slowly following his dad into the hall. This really was adding insult to flipping injury, or whatever the expression was. And this was no **minor** injury, either. **This** time, it could be flipping **terminal**.

CHAPTER 11

"You hungry, son?" said Norm's dad.

"What?" said Norm.

"It's a fairly simple question. You hungry? Yes or no."

Norm thought for a moment. His dad was right. It **was** a fairly simple question. Well, under **normal** circumstances it was a fairly simple question, anyway. In fact, under **normal** circumstances it was an abso-flipping-lute no-brainer. Because **normally** he'd have said yes, faster than you could say 'deep pan twelve inch Margherita from Wikipizza, with a side order of potato wedges and barbecue sauce'.

Because Norm **was**, without doubt, pretty flipping hungry by now. It was hardly surprising either. He hadn't had lunch. In fact, just about the only thing he'd had to eat all day were the Jammie Dodgers Grandpa had bought. And even **Norm** knew that a packet of Jammie Dodgers wasn't exactly a balanced meal. Not even if he had a packet in each hand. But these were **far** from normal circumstances. They'd gone vegetarian. Well, Norm had been **told** he'd gone vegetarian, anyway, which wasn't quite the same thing as far as he was concerned. Actually it wasn't anything **like** the same thing as far as he was concerned. But it appeared that he didn't have much say in the matter.

Now the question was, what horrors lay in store for him if he said yes? What would he be given to eat? He shuddered to think.

Nutrition facts

Serving size 128g

Amount per serving

Calories 420   122

%Daily value

Total fat 13.6g   21%

Nutritional value = 0%

"No need to look so **worried**, Norman."

That was easy for his **dad** to say, thought Norm.
Then again, it was easy for his dad to say
just about **anything**. Being a parent
had to be one of the easiest jobs in
the flipping **world**. All you ever did
was boss your kids around and get
them to do pointless stuff for you,
or else you just slobbed about,
watching whatever you wanted
on TV. Or in his mum's case,
slobbed about, buying loads
of completely useless stuff from
flipping shopping channels,
like left-handed flipping frying
pans, or solar-heated pants or
whatever. No flipping **wonder**
they didn't have two beans
to rub together!

"You're probably
wondering **why** I've
stopped outside a well-known
fast food outlet, when we're **supposed** to be
going to the supermarket," said Norm's dad.

205

Norm looked around. He hadn't even noticed that his dad had stopped the car, let alone that he'd stopped it outside 'a well-known fast food outlet'. And anyway why couldn't he have just said, McDonald's? It would have been much easier. And quicker.

"Well?" said Norm's dad expectantly.

"What?" said Norm distractedly.

"Why do you think I've stopped here, instead of the supermarket?"

Norm shrugged. "Dunno."

"To say, thank you."

Uh? thought Norm. His dad had stopped outside McDonald's to say **thank you**? Surely he could do that **anywhere**, couldn't he? And thank you, for what, exactly? What was he flipping **on** about?

"For doing what you did."

Norm pulled a face. "When?"

"At lunchtime," said Norm's dad.

"You mean..."

Norm's dad nodded. "When you told Danny to shut up."

"Riiiiiight," said Norm, **finally** beginning to understand.

"It took a lot of guts."

Really? thought Norm. Because he'd just blurted it out like some kind of uncontrollable burp. He couldn't have stopped it if he'd tried. But if his dad thought it had taken guts? That was fine by him.

Norm's dad seemed to hesitate slightly before carrying on.

"You know something else, Norman?"

Norm thought for a moment. He knew **lots** of things. But the odds of him knowing what his dad was going to say next were fairly slim.

"What, Dad?"

"I don't blame you."

Norm looked at his dad as if he'd just stepped off a spaceship. He wasn't being **blamed** for something? It was the oddest feeling ever. Because **normally** Norm got blamed for just about

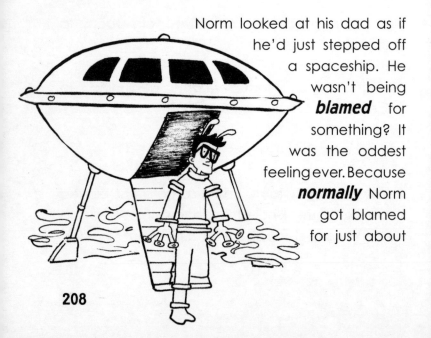

everything, from the state of the toilet after one of his brothers had just been in it, to the destruction of the flipping Amazonian rainforest.

"Are you sure, Dad?"

"Pardon?" said Norm's dad.

"Are you **sure** you don't blame me?"

Norm's dad chuckled. "Positive."

"But..."

"But nothing. I don't blame you. As a matter of fact, I'm quite proud of you."

Whoa, thought Norm. His dad was actually **proud** of him? If he'd known **that** was all it took, he'd have told Danny to shut up years ago!

"And I'll tell you something else for nothing," said Norm's dad.

"Yeah?" said Norm.

"It was actually quite funny."

Norm and his dad looked at each for a moment.

"Really?" said Norm.

"Really," said his dad, before breaking into the kind of face-splitting grin Norm hadn't seen since... Well, for as long as he could remember, basically. Which admittedly wasn't **all** that long. But he certainly hadn't seen his dad look this happy since before they'd moved house. Or rather, since before they'd **had** to move house.

"Honestly, Norman. The look on Auntie Jem's face? It was priceless! I don't think she could believe it. I don't think any of them could."

"But..." said Norm.

"What?" said his dad.

"I thought you'd be cross."

"Cross?" said Norm's dad. "It made my flipping **day**. If you'll pardon my language."

Norm suddenly burst out laughing. Partly out of relief. But mainly because it was so flipping unexpected, to hear his dad say **flipping**.

"I'm not joking, Norman. They were doing **my** head in, too."

"Right," said Norm.

"I couldn't say anything, though. But seriously. When **you** did? I could have **kissed** you."

Gordon flipping **Bennet**, thought Norm. He was glad his dad **hadn't** flipping kissed him. Not in front of his perfect cousins, anyway. Or in front of anyone for that matter. Because that was most **definitely** a step too far. He was nearly **thirteen**, for crying

out loud. And that was way too old for any kind of public display of emotion from his **parents**. Frankly that was too gross to even contemplate.

"So, what's it to be, then?"

"What do you mean, Dad?"

"I mean you can have anything you want," said Norm's dad.

"You mean..."

Norm's dad nodded. "To eat. Yes. Anything on the menu. It's yours. You choose."

By now, Norm had stopped laughing. When his dad said **anything**, did he really mean, **anything**?

"**Including** meat," said Norm's dad, as if he'd just read Norm's mind.

"WHAT?" said Norm, his eyes widening like saucers. "**Seriously**?"

"Of course," said his dad. "Just because we're vegetarian **in** the house doesn't mean we have to be vegetarian **out of** the house, now does it?"

Norm didn't say anything. He was too busy thinking about what he was going to order.

"Unless…"

"Unless what?" said Norm.

"Well, unless you'd actually **like** something vegetarian?" said Norm's dad. "It's entirely up to you really, Norman."

Right, thought Norm. Like he was actually going to **choose** something vege-flipping-tarian, when he could have literally **anything** he wanted? Well, anything on the **menu**, anyway. There was just one problem.

"What about Mum?"

"What about Mum?"

Norm stared at his dad, trying to figure out what he was saying. Or rather, what he **wasn't** saying.

"She doesn't need to know," said Norm's dad. "In fact – I don't **want** her to know, if you know what I mean, Norman?"

"You mean..."

"This is going to come out of the money I've got for shopping."

"Right," said Norm.

"So, we're going to have to...economise a little bit."

Economise? thought Norm. How were they going to do **that**? Everything they bought was already supermarket own-brand! Surely **nothing** was cheaper than **that**, was it?

"But **I** won't say anything, if **you** don't," said

Norm's dad. "Does that sound fair enough?"

Norm nodded until he thought his head was going to fall off. Not only did it sound fair enough, it sounded pretty flipping fantastic.

"This is our little secret, son."

Norm smiled. "Thanks, Dad."

"No. Thank *you*, Norman," said Norm's dad. "There's just one thing."

Flipping *knew* it, thought Norm. Why did there *always* have to be a thing? Why – just for once – couldn't there *not* be a thing?

"What, Dad?"

"We need to get a bit of a move on, if we don't want Mum to start getting suspicious."

"What?" said Norm. "Oh right. Yeah."

"Come on, then," said Norm's dad, getting out of the car and marching towards the entrance.

Norm watched him go and for a brief moment felt almost...almost... Well, almost...**affectionate** towards his dad. As if, for a split second in time, they'd actually been on the same wavelength as each other and shared some kind of bond. But he knew it wouldn't last. It never flipping did. And right now, Norm couldn't care less, either, because there was a burger with **his** name on it. And it **wasn't** going to eat **itself**.

"Norman?" yelled Norm's dad.

"Yeah?"

"Get a flipping shift on!"

"Coming, Dad!" Norm laughed, getting out of the car.

CHAPTER 12

Whether it was fate, or merely a coincidence, Norm would never know. Or ever care, for that matter. Because either way, Grandpa just happened to be getting off the bus as he emerged from McDonald's, milkshake in one hand and a whacking great burger in the other.

"Well, look who it is," said Grandpa. "My least favourite grandchild."

"Very funny, Grandpa," said Norm.

"No offence."

"None taken," said Norm. "Does that include Danny, Ed and Becky, by the way?"

"Naturally," said Grandpa, his eyes crinkling ever so slightly in the corners.

"Just checking," said Norm before taking a bite of his burger.

"That looks good," said Grandpa.

"It is," said Norm.

"Looks like a two-man job to me, Norman."

"What?" said Norm.

"Well, it's practically the size of your head," said Grandpa. "You're never going to manage it all on your own. Want me to help you out?"

"Nah, you're all right, thanks, Grandpa," said Norm before taking another bite.

"Suit yourself," said Grandpa. "Kids today."

Norm pulled a face. "Kids today, **what?**"

"That's it," said Grandpa. "Kids today."

Norm chuckled. Or at least **tried** to chuckle. But it wasn't easy, chuckling **and** munching a burger at the same time.

"With anyone?"

"With anyone **what?**" said Norm.

Grandpa sighed. "Are you **with** anyone?"

"Oh right," said Norm. "Yeah. My dad. He's still paying."

"Is he, now?" said Grandpa.

"Why?" said Norm.

"No particular reason," said Grandpa. "Just making polite conversation. I don't actually care."

"Charming," said Norm.

"Noticed anything, by the way?" said Grandpa after a few seconds.

Norm took a slurp of milkshake. He **hated** it when someone asked him that. Had he **noticed** anything? Not that he was asked it very often. But it happened often enough that it really **irritated** him whenever he **was**. Because he always felt like it was putting him on the spot. Like he was being **tested**. But it wasn't a big deal, noticing stuff. It wasn't like it was some kind of superpower. It'd be a pretty rubbish **superpower** if it was. And who cared if he'd actually noticed anything or not? Norm certainly didn't.

"Well?" said Grandpa. "**Have** you?"

Norm shrugged.

"This, for instance?" said Grandpa, holding up a bucket.

Great, thought Norm. So Grandpa was holding a bucket. What did he want? A flipping medal?

"Look familiar?"

Gordon flipping **Bennet**, thought Norm. Did it look **familiar**? It was a flipping **bucket**! What did Grandpa think he **was**? Some kind of **bucket expert**? If there was even such a **thing** as a flipping bucket expert. How many different sorts of buckets **were** there, for goodness' sake? Because they all looked pretty similar, as far as Norm was concerned.

"I'll tell you then, shall I?" said Grandpa.

"'Kay, Grandpa," said Norm, who was beginning to wish he'd stayed with his dad whilst he paid. It might have been *boring*, but it would have been nowhere *near* as boring as standing out here with Grandpa, talking about flipping *buckets*.

"It's the one you filled with snails," said Grandpa. "Or at least, half filled with snails."

"Really?" said Norm, feigning interest. "What are the odds?"

Grandpa looked at Norm for a moment. "Are you being sarcastic?"

"Yeah, a bit," said Norm.

"Noticed anything about it?"

Aw, *man*, thought Norm. Had he noticed anything about something he hadn't even noticed in the *first* place? Of *course* he flipping hadn't! This was starting to get seriously silly. As well as *seriously* annoying.

"Well?" said Grandpa. "Have you?"

Norm shook his head.

"It's empty."

Norm peered into the bucket. Grandpa was right. It **was** empty. But so what?

"It hasn't got a hole in it."

"Pardon?" said Norm.

"The bucket," said Grandpa. "It hasn't got a hole in it."

Norm genuinely didn't know what to say. Either he was being a bit slow to understand something, or Grandpa had lost the plot completely. Who flipping **cared** whether the bucket had got a hole in it, or not? What possible significance could that have?

"So?" said Grandpa.

"What?" said Norm.

"Where do you suppose they've gone?"

By now, Norm looked totally baffled. "Where do I think **what** have gone?"

"The **snails**!" said Grandpa. "What do you think I've **done** with them?"

"I honestly don't know, Grandpa," said Norm. Which was true. He honestly **didn't** know what Grandpa had done with the snails. Furthermore, he honestly had no interest whatso-flipping-**ever** in what Grandpa had done with the snails. Why **would** he? Grandpa had clearly confused him with someone **without** a life!

"I'll tell you then, shall I?" said Grandpa.

Norm sighed. "Whatever."

"Let's just say..." began Grandpa, before stopping again.

Norm could feel himself getting more and more impatient. Whatever it was that Grandpa was *just* going to say, he hoped that he was *just* about to say it quickly. Because at *this* flipping rate he was going to be ready for *another* head-sized burger before he'd finished flipping *saying* it.

"Let's just say, Auntie Jem might be needing a bit of extra help in the garden from now on."

Norm looked at Grandpa for a moment. "Sorry, Grandpa, what did you just say?"

"Remember when I said 'you scratch my back and I'll scratch yours'?"

Norm tried to think. *Did* he?

"You should do," said Grandpa. "It was only a couple of hours ago."

"Oh right, yeah," said Norm.

"You asked me how you could recycle snails," said Grandpa. "Well, not you personally. But in general?"

Actually, thought Norm, he really **could** remember that. It wasn't exactly something you were likely to forget in a hurry. Or even forget slowly. Even Norm. Not only that, but he was **beginning** to see where this conversation was heading.

"You mean..."

"Yep," said Grandpa, nodding. "They've found a new home. The snails, I mean. Not your cousins."

It took a few seconds to sink in. But as soon as it **had** sunk in, Norm started to smile.

"Yes, I had a feeling that might cheer you up," said Grandpa.

Cheer him up? thought Norm. Too flipping right it had cheered him up! What a stroke of sheer abso-flipping-lute *genius*! Why hadn't *he* thought of that?

"How did you do it, Grandpa?"

"Caught a bus there. Tipped them over the wall. Caught a bus back. Simple."

"Brilliant," said Norm.

"Glad you approve," said Grandpa.

"Approve of what?" said a voice.

Norm and Grandpa turned round to see Norm's dad heading their way, milkshake in one hand and a whacking great burger in the other.

"Well, look who it is," said Grandpa. "My least favourite son-in-law."

Norm's dad thought for a moment. "Hang on. I'm your *only* son-in-law, aren't I?"

"Exactly," said Grandpa, his eyes crinkling slightly in the corners.

"So?" said Norm's dad.

"So?" said Grandpa.

"You're glad that Norman approves of what?"

"The burger," said Norm quickly. Not that he thought his dad would mind if he knew what Grandpa had just done with the snails. In fact, knowing now how his dad felt about Auntie Jem and his perfect cousins, he was pretty sure that **he'd** approve, too! The problem was, he didn't want his mum to find out. And he knew that his mum and dad did occasionally talk to each other when he wasn't around. Or at least, he **presumed** they did, anyway.

"I see," said Norm's dad. "You won't say anything will you, Grandpa? To Linda, I mean?"

Grandpa looked at Norm and then at Norm's dad. "About the burger?"

"Yes," said Norm's dad. "We're supposed to be going vegetarian."

"**Vegetarian**?" said Grandpa. "My deepest condolences."

"Tell me about it," muttered Norm.

"I take it those aren't **veggie** burgers, then?" said Grandpa.

"Definitely **not**," said Norm's dad. "Just a little treat. But we'd rather no one knew about it, if you see what I mean?"

"My lips are sealed," said Grandpa.

"In fact," said Norm's dad, "we're **supposed** to be at the supermarket right now, not here stuffing our faces."

"Well, don't let me keep you," said Grandpa.

"Come on, you," said Norm's dad, getting back into the car.

"Good luck," said Grandpa as Norm did as he was told and got in the passenger seat.

But Norm didn't actually **care** what happened from now on. As far as **he** was concerned it had already been a completely flipping **brilliant** day, thanks largely to Grandpa and his bucket of lettuce-munching snails.

What could possibly go wrong?

CHAPTER 13

What could possibly go **wrong**? Well, in theory at least, **plenty** could possibly go wrong. In fact, in theory, just about **everything** could possibly go wrong. If you were **Norm** it could, anyway. Because that was just the way the cookie crumbled, in Norm's world. Or strictly speaking, that was just the way the supermarket own-brand Jammie Dodger crumbled, in Norm's world. Because for every teensy little up, there was almost inevitably a considerably bigger **down**. Life, for Norm, was like one long ride on a never-ending emotional roller coaster.

And besides, it wasn't even six o'clock by the time Norm and his dad had been to the supermarket and driven back home. The night was young. Norm certainly wasn't counting any chickens **just** yet. Not that Norm actually **had** any chickens to count. But that wasn't the point. The point was, there was still plenty of time for the day to go spectacularly pear shaped.

Except that for **once**, it really didn't look as if the day **was** going to go pear shaped, at all. Not that Norm was expecting everything to be wonderful all of a sudden, or to live happily after, like in some stupid fairy tale. But all that happened when he and his dad arrived back at the house was, well... not much, really. They just got out of the car and that was that. Chelsea didn't even automatically pop up on the other side of the fence, like some kind of nightmarish jack-in-the-box. It really was most peculiar. Not that Norm was complaining, of course. Well, not **yet**, anyway.

"Where do you think **you're** going?" said Norm's dad as Norm began heading straight for the front door.

"Who, me?" said Norm, stopping and turning around.

"Well, I don't see anyone **else** round here, do you?" said his dad.

Norm hated to admit it, but his dad did actually have a point. There **was** no one else round here. He could only have been talking to him.

"Well?"

"What?" said Norm.

"Are you going to give me a hand taking the shopping in, or what?"

"Uh?" grunted Norm as if his dad had just told him to hoover the street, blindfolded and with one hand behind his back.

"Well, you don't honestly expect me to do it all by myself, do you?"

Gordon flipping **Bennet**, thought Norm. So everything was well and truly back to flipping

normal, then? **That** hadn't taken long, had it? It was almost as if he'd **dreamt** the whole going to McDonald's and bonding over a burger with his dad, thing. As if it hadn't really happened at all.

"Well?" said Norm's dad. "Do you?"

"But..." began Norm.

"But what?" said Norm's dad.

Norm shrugged. "I was going to go **biking**."

"Well, you still **can**."

"**Really?**" said Norm, brightening ever so slightly.

"Of course," said his dad.

"Oh, right," said Norm.

"Just as soon as you've taken the **shopping** in."

Norm sighed.

"And once you've done the **recycling**."

"WHAAAAT?" squawked Norm like an outraged parrot.

"Well, have you **done** it yet?" said Norm's dad.

"No," said Norm. "But…"

"But nothing, Norman. You're doing it. And that's final."

"That is **SO** unfair," said Norm.

"Pardon?"

"THAT IS **SO** UNFAIR!" said Norm, much louder.

"I heard you the first time," said his dad.

So why get him to **repeat** it, then? thought Norm. Adults were **so** flipping weird sometimes.

"Why can't Brian or Dave do it, Dad?"

"Pardon?" said Norm's dad.

Norm looked at his dad, unsure whether to repeat himself or not.

"Why can't Brian or Dave do the recycling?" said Norm's dad.

Norm nodded. So his dad **had** heard him. **Again**.

"Because we asked **you** to do it, that's why!"

"Yeah," said Norm. "About **eight** hours ago!"

Norm's dad smiled. "Seriously?"

Norm thought for a moment, unaware that he wasn't exactly doing himself any favours and that if anything he was actually making things even **worse**. "Well, **about** eight hours ago. Maybe it was more like seven. I dunno, really. I didn't look at my watch. Well, I haven't **got** a watch. But I didn't look at my phone, anyway."

"You **do** realise that if you'd actually **done** the recycling eight hours ago, we wouldn't be having this conversation **now**, don't you?" said Norm's dad.

"Yeah, I know, but..." began Norm before stopping again. Even **he** could see that there was a certain amount of logic in what his dad was saying and that there probably wasn't any point in arguing any more. It was **so** flipping annoying.

"Do you want us to find you a few **more** jobs to do?" said Norm's dad.

"What?" said Norm. "**No!**"

"Because if you keep going like this I'll find you **plenty** of other jobs to do."

"Keep going like **what?**" said Norm.

"Like **this**!" said Norm's dad. "Now grab some bags, quick. Or else!"

Oh well, thought Norm, doing as he was told and grabbing a couple of carrier bags. It had been nice while it lasted, getting on with his dad. Just a pity it hadn't lasted a bit flipping longer, that was all.

"Hurry up, love!" said Norm's mum appearing at the front door.

"Why?" said Norm.

"What do you mean, **why**?" said Norm's mum. "Why **what**?"

"What's the hurry?" said Norm.

"Because I want to start making dinner, **that's** why!"

"Dinner?" said Norm. "I've only just..."

"Realised how hungry you are?" said Norm's dad, butting in quickly before Norm could finish the sentence himself.

"What?" said Norm.

"That's what you were about to say, wasn't it, Norman?" said Norm's dad. "That you've only just realised how hungry you are?"

"Oh right, yeah," said Norm after the very slightest of hesitations and twigging precisely **why** his dad was suddenly staring at him like a bug-eyed lunatic. Because of their little

secret. The secret that his **dad** didn't want his **mum** to find out about. Which, in turn, suddenly gave **Norm** an idea. If his dad **really** didn't want his mum to find out about them having a sneaky McDonald's, perhaps he might care to reconsider something.

"Are you **sure** I still have to do the recycling, Dad?"

"Pardon?" said Norm's dad.

This time, Norm knew that his dad had **definitely** heard him and that he was just stalling for time whilst he actually **processed** what he'd heard.

"It's just that..."

"Yes?" said Norm's dad. "Just that what?"

"Well, it's just that, if someone **else** did the recycling, it would mean I could go biking."

Norm and his dad looked at each other for a moment. Were they on the same wavelength as each other again? Were they **both** thinking what the **other** was thinking?

"Now you come to mention it, I suppose I **could** ask one of your brothers to do it instead," said Norm's dad.

"**And** any other jobs you were thinking of asking me to do?" said Norm.

"Yes, of course," said Norm's dad.

"For the next week?"

"A **week**?" said Norm's dad as if **Norm** had just told **him** to hoover the street, blindfolded and with one hand behind his back.

"Deal?" said Norm.

Norm's dad sighed. "Deal."

Result! thought Norm.

"Give me those bags," said his dad, the vein on the side of his head beginning to throb. Not that Norm noticed.

"What's going on?" said Norm's mum suspiciously.

"Nothing, Mum," said Norm breezily, giving his dad the carrier bags.

"Hmmm," said Norm's mum, as if she wasn't quite sure whether to believe Norm or not.

"Excellent," said Norm. "In that case I'll be a..."

"A what?" said Norm's mum.

"A...a...a..."

"Come on, Norman," said Norm's dad. "Spit it out! You'll be..."

"A...a...a...a...CHOOOOOOO!" went Norm.

"Oh dear, love," said Norm's mum. "Sounds like you've got a **cold** coming on.

"What?" said Norm. "No, it's just...a..."

"A what?" said Norm's dad.

"A...a...a...a...CHOOOOOOOOOO!" went Norm, even louder than before.

"I'm afraid that's definitely a cold, love," said his mum.

"Yes," said Norm's dad. "I bet that's because you got drenched when you put the washing out."

Yeah, thought Norm. *He* flipping bet it was as well!

"That's a pity," said Norm's mum.

"What do you mean?" said Norm.

"Well, you can't go biking now, love."

"WHAAAAAAAAAT?" yelled Norm. "You've got to be joking, right?"

But even as Norm said it, he **knew** that his mum **wasn't** joking – and that if she **was**, it was a pretty rubbish joke.

"Sorry, love," said Norm's mum.

"**You're** sorry?" said Norm. "How do you think **I** feel?"

"Don't be so cheeky, Norman!" said his dad.

"You're serious, Mum?" said Norm. "I really can't go biking?"

"It would be irresponsible if we let you, love."

Norm sighed wearily, as if he had the weight of the world on his shoulders. Irresponsible? More like unbe-flipping-***lievable***! And **so** un-flipping-fair.

But then, thought Norm, what was flipping ***new***?

Will life get less unfair for Norm?

 Will his two little brothers stop being so flipping annoying?

 Will Chelsea EVER just leave him alone?

THE WORLD OF
NORM
MUST END SOON

Find out in Norm's last laugh-out-loud adventure!

OUT MAY 2017

'Norm knew it was going to be one of those days text when he woke up and found himself about to pee in his mum's wardrobe...'

Want to read more? Abso-flipping-lutely!

Turn the page for a sneak peek of the first TWO chapters of

MUST END SOON!

CHAPTER 1

Norm knew it was going to be one of those days when he woke up and found himself about to pee in his mum's wardrobe. Not that he actually **knew** it was his mum's wardrobe. Or **anybody's** wardrobe, for that matter. All **Norm** knew was that he needed to pee. And pee was precisely what he intended to do.

"STOP!" yelled a voice.

Uh? thought Norm, still half asleep. Who was **that?** And what were they doing, watching him go to the flipping toilet? Couldn't a guy get **any** privacy around here?

"NORMAN!" yelled the same voice.

"Yeah?" croaked Norm, like a frog with laryngitis.

"What do you think you're **doing**, love?" said a different, gentler voice.

Norm thought for a moment. Firstly, just how many people were **in** the flipping bathroom? Secondly, what did he **think** he was doing? Or what was he **actually** doing? Was this some kind of trick question? Or just a really **stupid** one? Because either way, he still needed to pee. And if he **didn't** pee very soon, there was a good chance that he'd burst. And fourthly, what happened to thirdly?

Norm suddenly saw the light. Or, strictly speaking, Norm suddenly saw a **bedside** light, reflected in a mirror, a fraction of a second after it was switched on. Lying next to the light was Norm's mum. And lying next to his mum was his dad.

"Oh, hi," said Norm, turning around and finally realising where he was. And more importantly, where he **wasn't**.

"Never mind 'hi', said Norm's dad, grumpily. "Have you any idea what time it is?"

Time his dad bought a decent watch? thought

Norm.

"I'll tell you then, shall I? It's four o'clock in the morning! *That's* what time it is!"

Norm sighed. So if his dad knew what the time was all along, why flipping ask?

"This isn't the *first* time this has happened, Norman."

"It's the second time, actually," added Norm's mum, helpfully. "Except *last* time, it was your *dad's* wardrobe, not mine."

"'Snot *my* fault," muttered Norm under his breath.

"Oh, really?" said Norm's dad, the vein on the side of his head already beginning to throb – a surefire sign that he was getting stressed. Not that Norm noticed. Or *ever* noticed.

"Toilet's moved," muttered Norm.

"Pardon?" said Norm's dad.

"Toilet's moved!" said Norm, a little bit louder.

"'Snot where it used to be."

"I heard you the first time, Norman."

Gordon flipping **Bennet**, thought Norm. So why get him to repeat it, then? Was it **him**, or was his dad making even **less** sense than usual? And **that** was flipping saying something!

"I'm getting a strange sense of déjà vu, here," said Norm's dad.

That clinched it, thought Norm. His dad had started talking an entirely different language. He'd lost the plot completely. That's if he'd ever actually **had** the plot in the first place.

"We've had this conversation before," said Norm's dad.

"Almost word for word," said his mum.

"It wasn't the **toilet** that moved! It was us that moved!" said Norm's dad.

"Several months ago," said Norm's mum.

"Do you not remember, Norman?" said Norm's dad, sounding more and more exasperated.

Norm sighed. Did he remember having this conversation before? Or did he remember moving house? His dad really needed to be more specific.

"Well?" said Norm's dad.

Norm shrugged. "'Snot **my** fault."

"Will you **stop** saying that?" said Norm's dad.

"Well, it's not," said Norm.

"Well, it's certainly not **my** fault!" said Norm's dad.

"Huh," harrumphed Norm quietly. But not quite quietly enough.

"What was that?" said Norm's dad.

"It's OK," said Norm's mum, who, luckily, **could** tell when Norm's dad was getting stressed, and who was doing her best to act as peacemaker, as usual.

"No, it's **not** OK, actually," said Norm's dad. "Have you got something to say to me, Norman?"

Had he got something to **say?** thought Norm. To his **dad?** Where did he flipping start?

"Well?" said Norm's dad, expectantly. "I'm waiting."

Norm glanced at his mum, who, Norm couldn't help noticing, was staring back at him with what seemed to be an almost pleading expression in her eyes. As if she was trying to communicate something to him telepathically. As if she didn't want him to say whatever it was that he might be about to say.

"Can I go to the toilet?" said Norm.

Norm's dad sighed. "Off you go. And don't let this happen again."

Norm closed the wardrobe and headed for the door. He'd do his best to make sure it didn't happen again. But there was no guarantee.

CHAPTER 2

It was some time before Norm realised that he was awake. Or at least, until Norm **began** to realise that he was awake. Whether it was the shaft of sunlight penetrating the crack in the curtains and bouncing off his closed eyelids, or whether it was the gradual hum of activity from elsewhere in the house, Norm wasn't entirely sure. Not only that, but he didn't care, either. All Norm knew was that he was no longer asleep. Which was annoying for a start. Well, as far as **Norm** was concerned it was annoying, anyway. Because somewhere at the back of his mind, he was vaguely aware that he needed **more** sleep. That he somehow hadn't had **enough** sleep. That **something** had happened during the night, which had **interrupted** his sleep. But what?

Norm continued to lie in bed. Well, at least he

presumed it was his bed, anyway. But until he could actually be bothered to open his eyes and check, he wouldn't know for sure. There'd been that one time in IKEA when he lay down on a bed and the next thing he knew, he'd nodded off and had woken up to find a crowd of strangers staring at him, cooing and smiling, as if he was some kind of cute baby animal in a flipping zoo. His parents, on the other hand, hadn't found it cute at all. They'd been worried sick and told him in no uncertain terms not to go wandering off by himself again. Bit harsh, looking back on it now, thought Norm, because he must have only been about three at the time. But then, he'd also been an only child at the time, so he could understand his mum and dad being a **bit** anxious. Those were the days when **he** was the centre of their universe. Before his stupid little brothers came along and ruined everything for ever. Even so, it wasn't like he'd wandered off into the flipping **jungle** all by himself. The **biggest** danger he faced in IKEA was being bored to death. How his parents actually **enjoyed** going there, was beyond his comprehension. But then, his parents were in their forties. And people did weird stuff when they were that old.

There was a knock on the door. Which did little to improve Norm's mood. If anything, it made his mood even **worse**. Why did people have to knock on doors, anyway? They were **so** flipping annoying. Doors. Not people. Although thinking about it, thought Norm, thinking about it, people could be pretty flipping annoying too. Why couldn't they just leave him alone and not disturb him in the first place? Why did they always **want** things and need him to **do** stuff? And if they really had to disturb him, how about they make an appointment beforehand, instead of just turning up, unannounced? And how about they ring a flipping **bell**, instead of knocking?

"Can I come in, love?" said a muffled voice.

"I dunno," mumbled Norm. "**Can** you?"

Whether Norm's mum misheard Norm, or had decided to come in regardless, she opened the door and came in, anyway.

"Morning, sleepyhead."

"Are you sure?" said Norm, finally opening his eyes.

"Am I sure, **what?**" said Norm's mum, perching on the end of the bed.

"That it's morning?"

Norm's mum laughed. "Yes, I'm sure."

"Positive?"

Norm's mum nodded. "Positive."

"Prove it."

"Pardon?"

"Prove it," said Norm again.

"Prove what?" said Norm's mum.

"That it's morning."

"You want me to actually prove that it's morning?"

"Yeah," said Norm.

"How?"

Norm thought for a moment. "Dunno."

"Well, neither do I," said his mum. "You'll just have to take my word for it."

Norm yawned like a hippo. Not that he'd ever actually **seen** a hippo yawn before. But that wasn't the point. The point was that he was still tired.

Norm's mum smiled. "I take it you dropped off again, then?"

Dropped off? thought Norm. Dropped off what? And where? What was his mum on about?

"You got back to sleep?"

"Oh, right," said Norm, twigging. "Erm, yeah. S'pose so."

Norm's mum looked at Norm. "You don't remember, do you?"

Uh? thought Norm. He didn't remember **what?** The precise moment he went to sleep? Of course he didn't! What was he supposed to **do?** Take a flipping selfie, or something?

"Your nocturnal stroll?"

"My **what?**" said Norm.

"Your little night-time ramble?"

Gordon flipping **Bennet**, thought Norm. Why couldn't she just say whatever she was **trying** to say, instead of talking like she'd swallowed a flipping **dictionary?**

"When you nearly ..."

"Nearly **what?**" said Norm.

"Peed in my wardrobe?"

"Uh?" said Norm. "I did **what?**"

"Nearly peed in my wardrobe. You stopped just in time."

"Seriously?"

Norm's mum nodded. "Seriously."

So *that* was what had happened during the night, thought Norm. He *knew* there was something. He just couldn't remember what it *was*.

"Soooo …"

"What?" said Norm.

"You don't remember the conversation you had with your dad, either, then?"

"When?" said Norm.

"At four o'clock this morning."

Norm pulled a face. If he couldn't remember peeing in his mum's wardrobe at four o'clock this morning – or rather, *nearly* peeing in his mum's wardrobe at four o'clock this morning – he was hardly likely to remember a flipping conversation he had with his dad at four o'clock this morning, was he?

"What was it about, Mum?"

"Doesn't matter," said Norm's mum.

Uh? thought Norm. So if it *didn't* matter, what was the flipping point of *mentioning* it, then?

"It's just that …"

Just that what? thought Norm. His mum seemed reluctant to continue. But eventually she did.

"You shouldn't be *too* quick to blame him."

"Sorry, what, Mum?" said Norm, by now more than just a tad confused.

"For moving," said Norm's mum.

"Moving?" said Norm.

"House," said his mum. "Don't be *too* quick to blame your dad."

Too *quick?* thought Norm. What did she mean, too *quick?* First of all, they'd moved house ages ago. And second of all, it *was* his flipping dad's fault. After all, it was his *dad* who'd lost his job, not him.

It was his dad who'd blown loads of money, not him. As far as **Norm** was concerned, his dad was a **hundred** per cent responsible for them having to move. If not more.

"Do you not think he feels bad enough already?" said Norm's mum.

Norm shrugged. Or at least **tried** to. But it wasn't easy, shrugging whilst lying in bed. And anyway, what kind of ridiculous question was **that?** How was he supposed to know how his **dad** felt? Norm knew how he felt. He felt angry. Angry because they'd had to leave their **old** house. Angry because he never had any money to pimp up his mountain bike. Angry because he was expected to eat supermarket own-brand Coco Pops for the rest of his flipping life, instead of **proper** Coco Pops like before. Angry because ... because ... well, because things just weren't like they used to be. Not that things were ever particularly **amazing** before. They were never, ever rich beyond Norm's wildest dreams. That would be impossible. And it wasn't like they used to live in a massive palace, or anything. It was a pretty normal house. But a pretty normal-**sized** house. With normal-sized rooms. It wasn't like they used to be loaded. But compared to **now?** It seemed like another world. Another galaxy. Another flipping universe.

"Well, I'll tell you," said Norm's mum. "He does feel bad. And the last thing he needs right now is for anyone to **remind** him."

Great, thought Norm. He hadn't even got out of bed yet and already he was being lectured. Didn't exactly bode well for the rest of the flipping day, did it?

Norm's mum smiled. Or at least **tried** to. "Things can only get better, love."

"Can I have that in writing?" said Norm.

"I understand your frustration."

Norm pulled a face. "Really?"

"Of course," said his mum. "I was your age once, you know."

Norm looked at his mum for a moment. He seriously

doubted she was ever his age.

"So?" said Norm's mum.

"What?" said Norm.

"Are you going to get up at some point?"

"Do I have a choice?" said Norm.

"Oh, come on, love. It's not *that* bad, is it?"

Not yet, thought Norm. But the day was still young.

Don't miss

to find out what happens next!

THE WORLD OF NORM

MAY BE RECYCLED

HELLO, NORM FANS.
DO YOU WANT TO WIN SOME STUFF FOR YOUR BIKE?
PLUS SOME NORM GOODIES?

- Go to the World of Norm website at: www.worldofnorm.co.uk

- Enter the competition

- You may win a prize!

BLING!

Closing date: 31st January
See website for full
terms and conditions.

Don't forget, kids,
Norm will return in...

THE WORLD OF
NORM

MUST END SOON

Don't miss his LAST
laugh-out-loud adventure!

OUT MAY 2017

www.worldofnorm.co.uk

ORCHARD BOOKS
Illustrations © Donough O'Malley